Casting In Stone

A Novel of the Averraine Cycle

By Morgan Smith

Traveling Light Publications
ISBN: 978-1523997046

This book is a work of fiction. Nothing in this is remotely based on actual events nor does it take place in any earthbound locale. None of the characters or situations has even a smidgen of reality about them, nor did I write it to get back at my legion of enemies or my arch-nemesis. If you see yourself in one of the characters, you either need a stiff drink, a change in your medication, or a long, hard look in the mirror.

Cover design and artwork by Mandi Schrader. Photographer: Rod Heibert. Model: The Partially Examined Wife. Many thanks to Dark Ages creations for loaning the armour and weapons. If anyone is in Calgary and needs a nice chainmail shirt, those are the people to see!

Table of Contents

Prologue

News comes late and slowly here, when it comes at all.

But there were two missives today, brought to me by the last traders, stragglers working their way through the valley before the snows come. One was from the Reverend Mother, approving my request to stay on permanently in Rhwyn. I could sense her puzzlement, though. She wants a further explanation, and I cannot give it to her.

The other was about the babe. Born weeks too early, it seems, but hale enough, nonetheless. It was the old man who sent word, and he has questions, no doubt, and suspicions, aye. He's a canny one, though, and he couched it all in unexceptional words. Nothing outright, nothing that could alarm anyone, but he knows something is wrong, that's plain enough. He puts it down to that old stand-by, a hard birthing giving rise to the sad-mother sickness. It's common enough. But underneath the careful phrases, I could sense his disbelief and his disquiet. She hadn't been easy, he wrote, even before she was brought to bed.

What can I say? Mayhap time will ease their anger. If they can just keep their secrets, if they do not shout from every hilltop what a poor, misbegotten creature we wrought, if the Goddess has a care for the babe - it might yet come aright.

Chapter One

The silence was vast, broken only by the sporadic sobbing breaths of the woman crouched over that little, twisted body.

I watched the villagers with interest. As neighbours, they were usually a dull lot, but their reactions to this tragedy needed comprehension. The corpse was not pretty, and they were doing their level best not to look too closely. One of the women was kneeling beside the child's mother, trying to offer comfort.

Her heart wasn't in it, though. Even from a distance, her tense shoulders and shadowed eyes shouted soundlessly what every one of them was thinking.

"Thank the Goddess, it wasn't one of mine!"

I understood that. You couldn't blame them, it might easily have been one of theirs, after all. It already had been and likely would be again, if someone didn't do something soon.

They were grateful when Eardith arrived, brisk and business-like, but with that rough sympathy they understood. She was strong, opinionated, stern and forthright, all qualities that would have given her nothing but trouble in a larger, more sophisticated place. People in those places are accustomed to having their priests excuse their little transgressions quietly. Eardith's advice and solace tended to come with a bracing dose of sarcasm and common sense.

I had shared her cottage peaceably for nearly three years. She didn't pry, she didn't gossip, and, luckily for me, she never refused to assist anyone in need.

She looked at me over the mother's bowed head, and I just nodded. Yes, it was pretty much the same as the other ones. No, I had no idea how to prevent it.

Lord Owain and his forester Joss came around the side of the village's only inn, looking grim. Owain went straight to the women by the little corpse, resting a hand on the mother's shoulder in helpless sympathy.

"Something," said Eardith, "will have to be done."

Well, that was obvious. It was the third such incident in less than a seven-day. There was a fresh grave already for Briega's next-to-youngest, and Gair's daughter was lying ripped and nigh-on bloodless, barely clinging to life. Folk murmured that she was a lucky one, but I wasn't so sure. If she lived, which seemed unlikely, it would be with a scarred face and a useless leg along with the memory of a savage and horrific attack.

Joss had stopped by Eardith, whispering something swift in her ear. Her reaction was neither helpful nor promising: she merely looked, if it were possible, more shuttered and bleak than ever.

Owain, having nothing he could do for the grieving, began to organize the removal of the body, and issuing orders for caution, patrolling, not letting the youngsters out on their own, all of which had been said from the start. What could you do? A toddler waking in the night and creeping out to use the latrines wasn't something you could prevent, not really.

Gradually, the crowd dwindled, the women rallying around the bereft parents and bearing them off to the inn, a few of the men coming back with a hurdle to carry the little scrap of dead humanity off to the shrine. In the end, it was only Joss, Owain and Eardith left.

And me. They were all looking at me.

I was, for all intents and purposes, the only armed and mildly dangerous person here, and I filled no identifiable village role. I was easily the most expendable person they knew.

"Wolf scat, up towards the ridge," Joss said. "Like the others. But there are three, not two, this time."

Wolves don't do this, I thought. Wolves don't walk into a village and wait patiently, night after night, for human prey. But Joss was a woodsman, through and through. He knew as well as I did we were not dealing with ordinary wolves.

Hungry ones might, I supposed, go after a child out alone. But it had been a mild enough winter and an early, pleasant spring. The hills were teeming with game. We had untouched sheep in the pens and unmolested hens in the coops, if it came to that. And the children had not been eaten, merely savaged and left.

A rabid wolf might go after a child. One rabid wolf, maybe, but rabid wolves do not act in groups, and a rabid animal is not usually given to patience or patterns. This was becoming all too predictable.

"Lady Caoimhe?" This was Lord Owain, and I didn't need for him to spell it out.

"Right."

I knew what they wanted. There was no good reason I knew of for me not to give it to them.

"Joss, you'll go with her." Owain wasn't very good at giving orders, they always came with the faintest of questioning tones trailing in at the end, but Joss was used to this and just shrugged.

Eardith was already moving off, down towards the path leading to the shrine. I caught Joss's eye, said "A half-glass, and we can meet at the crossroads," and trotted after her, catching up as the path led off into the trees.

I didn't speak. Eardith, if she wanted to tell me anything, would do so in her own time, and I was never one for asking questions, anyway. Instead, I listed in my head the things I needed: hunting spears, my long knives, something to eat in case we were out past midday…

What I liked about Joss mainly was his silence. Occasionally we hunted together, or in high summer, took a little boat out onto the lake and fished. Beyond noting some form of imminent weather change or remarking on tracking potential, we rarely spoke, and that suited me. What happened in the village, the endless litany of who was angry or in love with whom, or who was a lazy sod or a lucky one - I couldn't see what any of it had to do with me or why I should care. I just lived here, on a probably temporary and barely tolerated scrap of allowance that Eardith's authority had allotted me.

When I got to the crossroads, where the cart track threading north through Rhwyn met the road west to Davgenny, he was squatting by the evidence the wolves had left behind, but he rose soundlessly and headed to the little trail that veered back into the hills, halting only to wordlessly point out the signs that they had passed here as well.

It looked almost as if the wolves had stopped to have a conference. There were three depressions that spoke of animals sitting for some time, prone and indolent in last year's dead grass. There were paw-prints that circled, as if at least one of them had paced restlessly, bored by some vulpine debate.

I squinted up into the mountains beyond Rhwyn Vale, where mist still clung to the trees.

There was an overgrown and unused twisty little pass out of Camrhys somewhere above us, theoretically a concern for Lord Owain, but far too small and too treacherous to accommodate more than a really courageous mountain goat or a desperate fugitive with nothing to lose. Owain scarcely heeded it. Certainly there was no organized effort at patrols: he hadn't the manpower.

If he'd sometimes hinted that my attention there might be welcome if I cared to put the effort in, Fardith had rather discouraged me from venturing into the mountains too much. The pass was of no use to anyone, she said, and a solitary traveller could easily come to grief out there.

The wolves - if wolves they were - disagreed. The signs pointed resolutely eastward and upward out of the valley.

Chapter Two

Technically, I was Joss's overlady.

To be perfectly exact, I was Lord Owain's overlady, simply because of a thoughtlessly bestowed bride-gift, although Owain had never once given any indication that he was aware of who or what I was. He called me "Lady" out of simple good manners and neither he, his wife nor anyone else in Rhwyn behaved as if I was anything more than a stranger who had stumbled into their midst. Someone Eardith had given sanctuary and a quasi-legitimate place to, for reasons she had not shared. I hadn't intended this as my destination, and it was a good couple of weeks after I'd arrived that I became aware myself that I owned this valley.

So, when we came to where the wolf signs ran out, still pointing inexorably east up into the heights, and Joss turned to me and asked, diffidently, what we ought to do next, I was mildly surprised. I had expected him to either remain in charge or to abandon me to whatever the wolves had in store. Instead, it seemed as if he expected me to determine his fate, and that was odd.

The kindest thing, I thought, was to send him back. Whatever we were tracking wasn't ordinary or safe, I was fairly sure of that. But if we were to have any hope of ending this disagreeable interlude, two people likely had a better chance than one.

Hells, if we were to have any chance of picking up their trail out along the rocky terrain ahead, I needed Joss, who had that peculiar intuition that all good woodsmen have, that uncanny ability to out-think any animal and anticipate their actions.

"They're up there somewhere. With luck, we can find their lair and make an end of it."

Joss gave me a mildly exasperated look. The wolves would hear and smell us miles before we came across them. I just shrugged. It wasn't as if there was some better plan in the offing.

A glass or two later, I was beginning to think better of this. We had worked our way out of the thinning trees and traversed an expanse of rocky scrabble only to come up against a sheer drop of a deep gorge that seemed to extend for miles. The only way around appeared to be looping back towards the tree-line and heading further east where the rift veered away from what seemed to be, from this distance, a wooded slope up towards that unusable pass.

When we made it that far, the trees were dark and closely ranked, blotting out almost all of the sunlight, and the silence lay on us, heavy and unsettling. Every footfall echoed. It had been long and long since people had come this way.

There were faint signs that we were on the right track, though. At least there were according to Joss. I had the minimum hunting skills anyone in my position would have had, in that the more obvious evidence was clear to me, and I could move soundlessly enough not to be a hindrance. The tiny changes and infinitesimal clues that Joss relied on were out of my league, though.

At some point well past mid-day, we stopped to pull out packets of bread and cheese and to rest in that oppressive silence. Far off, I could hear the faintest echo of a brook or rivulet tumbling over rocks, but that was all I could hear, beyond our own breathing. No wind stirred the branches overhead, no sunlight filtered through the dim of the shade and no birdsong enlivened the air. It was, as they say, as quiet as the grave, and rather nearly as chilly.

After a bit, we went on, threading our way among the trees in an erratic route governed by those indefinable traces Joss seemed to see, still eastward and more or less upward ever higher towards the slim break between two scarred peaks that signaled what had once been a pass. It had only ever been suitable for smaller pack-trains and roaming bands of less than competent bandits across a now highly contested border. Rock falls had closed this pass long ago, if I remembered correctly; rock falls and laziness on the part of those traders and outlaws who had just moved on to use other passes or given up trying altogether.

Joss stopped so suddenly, I almost walked into him. I had just enough awareness not to grunt out loud in surprise, but peered into the gloom ahead.

There: the slightest moving shadow among deeper shadows. I didn't dare so much as breathe, mentally cursing at my own unreadiness and reversing my grip on my spear, and then carefully easing back a step as smoothly and quietly as I could. Joss, at least, had not been as careless. His hand slid to the quiver at his hip and slid an arrow out, suddenly nocked and ready in one swift movement.

I felt, rather than heard the beginning of a growl behind me and whirled, crouching instinctively, just as an enormous gray shape hurtled towards me. My spear came up just in time to catch the beast at the shoulder, throwing him off course as the tip glanced away down his side, and the shock of that weight wrenched the shaft from my hands. I heard the whistle of an arrow behind me and then an uncharacteristic curse from Joss and the *thunk!* as something connected with a tree-trunk.

There was a snarl from the trees, the sound of branches crackling, and then, as suddenly as they had come, they were gone.

Joss was still kneeling, another arrow nocked and ready. I retrieved my spear.

"Well, they aren't stupid," I said. Joss shook his head, and rose, still watchful. He seemed angry, although with someone like Joss, it's hard to tell.

"Is it worth going on?" I asked. "I mean, we won't be surprising anything now."

"Den can't be far off," he said, finally. "No point in stopping now."

"Fair enough. But do me a favour? Don't get hurt. I swear I won't carry you back down if you do."

He grinned. "You, neither."

After a while, it seemed as though the trees began to thin, although we still walked in shadow. The early spring had not penetrated this far and there was a fair bit of snow in patches against the gnarled, exposed tree roots.

We came to a place where the rock began to reassert itself through the soil, great walls of granite where scrubby bushes clung desperately to tiny footholds in the crevices and we passed into a kind of ravine of smooth, grey stone walls reaching up towards the sky and yet there was no more light here than when we had walked among the trees below.

I stopped, frowning. There was something not quite right about this. The rocks were too smooth, too even, there were small stone piles that seemed just a bit too regular, too deliberately placed to be natural, and a sense of vague familiarity was tugging at me, like a housecat begging to be let out to mouse.

For just a moment my vision wavered. Things shivered and blurred at the edges and then, just as suddenly, they stilled, and I caught a strange, fugitive chill of something being about to break, wide and wild.

My hands were moving to my belt and pulling out my long knives without bidding, and they were on us, leaping down from a rocky ledge hidden by a few bits of bush and the shadow of the stony ridge above.

One knife, by some lucky chance, caught the first one perfectly at the heart, but I went down under the weight, losing my breath and precious seconds in the process. There was a roaring in my ears and blood everywhere and I heaved at the wolf carcass, half-crawling and half-rolling out from under, wondering if I was too late for Joss.

He was still standing, though he'd abandoned the bow and was fending off a second huge grey beast with the spear I'd loaned him, his back against the rocks, and blood dripping from his left arm. I tucked my feet under me and lunged toward the wolf, yelling, in the vain hope of distracting it.

The sound and the movement worked, just a little. The wolf slid its gaze just that hair sideways and Joss, Goddess love him, jammed the spear down his gullet. The reacting rage and convulsively renewed attack flung Joss brutally against the rocky ground, but he hung on, somehow keeping the wolf at bay, until the damage caught up to it and it sank, whimpering and gushing blood, onto the ground.

For one long moment, it was as if the world caught its breath, more still than death.

And then I thought of the third wolf and looked up, scanning the rocky walls around us. Behind me, Joss drew a struggling breath, wheezy with the effort and I thought idly he must truly be in some pain or he would have never made a sound.

I was already reaching for his bow and fumbling for an arrow without conscious thought when a vague smudge beside an oddly shaped tumble of rocky scree resolved itself into a massive grey hulk, gathering its force under it, the biggest wolf I had ever seen, or even heard of.

I needed three grains of the glass, but I only had two, I reckoned. Still, I drew my breath and held it, and thought hard about aim.

The wolf was already in motion as my arm pulled back, mid-air and nearly on me when the arrow released.

But that's the thing about a pointblank shot. Even I could not fail to hit a beast that big, straight on and squarely in its chest.

There is always that moment, when a danger is past, where the world seems a better place than it did before. The miraculous continuance of one's own life lends a kind of sweetness to the reality, a mix of relief and remembrance, melting into a giddy gladness and a celebratory mood.

Or so I'm told: my own reactions had always been less intense, and infinitely more cautious, but generally, I understood the theory.

This time I felt not even a hint of faint joy in finding myself still on this side of the grave. Nor did Joss, I guessed. He groaned and sagged to the ground, still dripping blood. I retrieved my knife where I'd dropped it in my scrabble for the bow and cut away at my shirt hem to make a clumsy bandage for him, filled with a curious sense of urgency to be gone and far away from this rocky, barren place and these three wolf corpses.

Then I felt it.

The faintest of tremors, just the once.

Imagination? No, there it was again, just the tiniest bit stronger.

Once more, and this time it was a trembling in the ground that I truly felt, as if the rocks were somehow settling deeper into their place, bracing themselves against who knows what.

But that was suddenly the least of my concerns. I could have forgotten that moment. I would have forgotten it.

The wolf I had killed, the big one…shimmered, outlines hazy, and I swear for just a moment I saw a man there, as eerily beautiful as evil ever could be, and his eyes alive and triumphantly malevolent, staring at me as if to memorize my features for some future day…

And then, nothing.

The wind rose and fell again with a tired sigh, and the animal corpses, the rocks and the trees were all once more utterly and completely ordinary, inanimate and without menace.

Joss said nothing, his eyes wide and fixed on me. He watched me bind him up without so much as a word, struggling to his feet to help me collect our bits of scattered gear and then taking the lead in our slow journey back down the hillside.

We didn't look back at that uncanny place. Our eyes and thoughts were firmly on leaving, eager, the pair of us, to be back in our village. It wasn't until we'd gained the deeper woods that it occurred to me that the day was nearly spent and that we were too far out to think of safe hearth-sides, warm dinners and mugs of ale just yet.

So we found a spot sheltered by a fallen tree and a bit of stony hillside, and I gathered firewood while Joss rummaged one-handedly in his scrip and produced a bit of dried meat and a few crusts. My contribution was the leather flask of raisin wine I'd absentmindedly packed for midday and then forgotten.

We ate what little we had, and I passed him the flask, all without more than a grunt or two to indicate what needed doing next.

"You've nerves, you have," Joss said suddenly. "You'd not a moment to spare or room to think in - I'd have cut and run, I would."

It was possibly the longest speech I'd ever heard him volunteer. Blood loss must be making him delirious. I pointed out that I'd not had much choice, and that the closer the wolf was, the better my chances, anyway.

He shook his head.

"And I thought you were for leaving me, if I was hurt," he said, as if this clinched something.

"Your legs still work. And to be honest, your mother is scarier than any wolf. I didn't fancy telling her I'd dropped you off as a bad bet."

***

In the morning, the world seemed a safer, friendlier place. Even a little of the weak, early sun began to make its way through the trees a bit as we stifled the last embers of our fire, gathered our gear and headed at a gentle pace down towards home.

Once there, we were met by the unsurprising news that Gair's daughter had died in the night.

Our killings were received with some relief, although I felt bound to point out that we could not be absolutely sure all danger was past. There could be more wolves. No one really wanted to think about that, not even Eardith, seemingly, although she coaxed every detail of our encounter from me.

More, in fact: I found myself telling her things I wasn't aware of at the time.

He had been wearing a long, dark blue tunic with even darker embroidery at the cuffs, the man-wolf. Circles and stars in deep, deep blue, eerily similar to the marking of the soldiers and servants of the royal house of Camrhys.

Possibly, Eardith said, a runaway criminal who made it through the pass. I don't know why she thought this was reassuring. A man who was a wolf? That sound and vibration? It did not seem to me that anything at all had been resolved, and I could see that beneath her calm, Eardith was puzzled, and wary, too. With no further explanation forthcoming, though, all I could do was to be vigilant.

But the days slipped by and no more signs or calamities occurred. The village rebounded, mourned their dead and buried them, and became occupied with springtime traditions.

There was a festival to plan for, and the first of the traders coming north to look forward to. In the meantime, the village got on with planting crops and gardens, the shearing and the repairs from winter's depredations on roofs and fences. We fell into the usual seasonal rounds and chores, as familiar and as ordinary as breathing.

I continued to wake before dawn, going out to the back of Eardith's tiny garden and running through warm-up stretches and pointless sword drills as the sun rose, then chopping the day's wood and hauling water from the spring. I ate, I cared for the animals, and then, if I wasn't drafted into some communal chore the villagers needed all hands for, I ran through more pointless drills, cared for my unused weapons, saddled my horse and hunted, or merely walked the woods and meadows aimlessly.

The weather had been variable in the days after the wolves, keeping me close to home. One morning finally brought a light mist and Joss turning up with the offer of a day's fishing. The thought of something beyond last autumn's dried meat and wrinkled turnips for supper was irresistible.

It was one of those days. The sun chased away the damp, the fish were co-operative, the company and the exercise of rowing, along with the concentration required, were just enough to still my thoughts. I felt satisfied and calm as I walked back to the cottage, three good trout in my creel, and thinking how pleasant it might be to go on like this forever.

There were two horses tethered on the grassy verge outside Eardith's cottage, and one of them was a horse I knew.

I ought to have turned south, I thought. I ought to have left that first morning, rainstorm or no, and gone south to Glaice. Better still, I ought to have sold my horse in Dungarrow town and bought passage on some trader ship bound for Fendrais, or Raeth, or Istara, even, and sold my skills to the highest bidder.

Too late for weeping now, I thought, and pushed open the cottage door.

Chapter Three

Eardith was sitting in her usual place on a box chair that had a hard back, her single concession to her years. It had been a gift from Owain, who considered her utterly ancient and wise, although in fact she was no more than fifteen years or so his elder and quite the halest woman in the village.

On the long bench beside the hearth there was a young woman, barely out of girlhood, wearing the marks of a priestess like Eardith, but fresh and clean and unworn and with a faint consciousness, as if they were new and dearly bought.

It was her companion sitting beside her who had my attention, though.

He was smiling. I knew that smile. He had smiled just that way too many times for me to misread him. It was when Guerin of Orleigh looked his most benign that one had the most to fear.

"Oh, hullo, Caoimhe," he said, without the least hint that he hadn't merely been passing through and dropped in by chance.

The reaction of the girl beside him was instant, though. She stiffened, as if her spine had turned suddenly to stone, looking first at Guerin and then at me. Long and hard and narrowly at me.

"Hullo, Guerin. How are things?"

His smile deepened. "Nothing outrageous lately. But surely the news comes to you here, however slowly?"

I smiled back. Two could play this game. "You know me, though. Always the last to hear the gossip."

"What a shocking liar you are, Caoimhe. You always know everything - you just never care enough to remember it. But let me introduce Lady Arlais, who you will not know, being so long from Dungarrow. Arlais, this is Lady Caoimhe, a longtime…friend."

The girl looked so stiff I thought she might break if she moved, but she inclined her head in my direction in a skimpy nod. "Indeed," she said tonelessly, "her name, at least, is not unknown."

I imagined not. But she was already turning her attention back to Eardith.

"We will need to speak further," she said. "When it is," here she flicked an irritated glance my way again, "more convenient."

I can count on my shield hand how many people I truly admire in this world. Eardith might well have been the top of my list that day: she looked over Lady Arlais with the same expression she had when she perused late season vegetable marrows in the marketplace, and said,

"My dear girl, there is no point at all in keeping a secret from the one actual witness you have. If you wish to discuss the incident I reported to the Reverend Mother and to His Grace, you need to discuss it with Caoimhe, who was there. And," here she held up a hand, forestalling an apparent imminent outburst from Arlais, "do not speak to me of trust or any such fol-de-rol. Caoimhe is the last person to report on anything other than the actual facts, such as they are. That is all that matters."

"With all due respect," said Arlais, angrily, "I do *not* trust her. I cannot. I wonder at you, Lady Eardith."

"I think I am old enough not to have a child question my judgment. I know Caoimhe well enough. Speak to her or not: it is your journey wasted if you choose. I told all I could in my letter, and I have nothing to add."

"You know her well enough? Do you truly think so? Did you know that she is a known oathbreaker and a murderer?"

Arlais' face was quite pink, with some kind of third-hand rage and shocked propriety, as if she represented some great moral authority. I suppose, by her lights, she did.

She turned to me. "I've no doubt you spun some tale of woe and cozened this poor lady into keeping you safe from justice!" she said nastily. "I've heard all the tale, however: how you ignored the Duke's direct orders and murdered your own husband in cold blood. And how your poor sister you were so jealous of took her own life in shame of your deeds!"

Suddenly, I was quite angry. It's one thing to have a past. It's another to have some complete stranger throw it in your face.

"Is that the tale they tell on the holy isle? Is that how your education was, full of whispered scandals and half-truths? I suppose they don't mention that my poor sister was only eleven years old, hadn't even had her Goddess-night. Or that my husband raped her, and she killed herself because she thought she was spoiled in the eyes of the Goddess because of that? She was dead two full days before Feargal…"

I stopped. I looked at Eardith. "She is right about one thing, though. I did murder Feargal, for all it was judicial combat. And Einon asked me not to. It wasn't an order, but… I am a murderer, in any way that matters."

"I know, dear." Eardith said, comfortably. "You told me the tale the very first night. You said you wouldn't take charity under false pretenses."

"Did I? I don't remember…" But then I did, wet, cold and exhausted I'd been and still half-mad with grief.

The room grew silent. Arlais looked shocked and bewildered, the ground cut out from under her feet, seemingly. My anger washed away as suddenly as it had come. She had only spoken as she knew, after all, and what reason had I to think that justice and fairness ruled in this world?

"I'll see to these fish of mine," I said, heading back towards the door. It banged shut behind me.

In the sunlight, it all seemed even more pointless. Who was I defending? Meryn? A dead child could not possibly care what retribution I took. If the priests spoke true, she was with her Goddess now. If they lied, well, dead was dead, and nothing could harm her further. And lashing out at some ignorant young priestess filled with a cracked version of dire events woven on the loom of romance into a web of pleasurable censure - that would not change a thing.

Meryn was dead. Feargal was dead. I was dead, too, for all intents and purposes, if indeed, I had ever actually lived. The Goddess loves to do things in threes.

I was just starting to gut the last fish when the door opened and Arlais came out. To her credit, when she came up to me, she did not sniff or recoil from the mess on the ground.

Indeed, she looked pale and shamefaced. I tried to pretend my eyes were all for my fish. It seemed even more to me now that she was a poor target for my demons: an untried girl sent to do some task and terrified of doing it wrong.

"Lord Guerin says I am to apologize," she said in a small voice.

"Really? And you listened to him? I never do."

She made a small sound somewhere between a snort and a giggle.

"Is it true, what you said?"

"She wanted to be a priestess," I said, after a moment. "She seemed meant for it, all her life. And he took that from her. At least, she believed so."

"No one at Braide ever said..." Her voice trailed off.

"Well," I pointed out, "it made a better tale, the way they told it. More like what the bards sing of, anyway."

She could have just gone in then. I wouldn't have minded. This wasn't a conversation I wanted to have.

But Arlais, having decided I was not, after all, one of the Dark Incarnates personified, was on a bit of a private mission here.

"They say you are the best swordhand in all Keraine. That you never lose. That you can kill without thinking. Is it true?" She was looking me over with a critical eye.

"Does it truly matter to you to know?"

She said, "You aren't as tall as some. You don't look stronger than anyone else your size. Are you just faster? Or know more tricks?"

I smiled. "I do know a few tricks, but that isn't why. Or at least, it isn't the main reason."

"Well, then?"

I let the smile fade. "Most people define winning and losing differently than I do, that's all."

Arlais frowned. "What does that mean?"

"Look you," I said. "Every person I have ever fought defined winning as my death, and their life. Every other person in a dueling ring or on a battlefield measures their success by the fact that they are alive at the end of it. They define their loss by their death. And I don't. I define success only by my opponent's death. That's all."

"I still don't -"

"I don't mind if I die," I said flatly. "As long as they're dead, I've won. My own life can end as well, I don't mind." I paused. She looked quite shocked. "You would not believe the number of options that gives me in a fight."

Chapter Four

I don't remember if there was ever a time when I did not know my parents hated me.

There must have been. Children cling to the hope of their parents' love long after the illusion's been shattered, and I don't think that as a babe, I was so different from any other. It was the constant reinforcement of Kevern's loathing, especially, and my mother's cross between indifference and support of his brutality towards me that must have worn through my hopes and dreams.

All I remember is their hatred, though. No one loved me, and although my grandfather tried to shield me from too early a comprehension of my lot, no one, not even he, seemed to like me much. The best I got was toleration, the worst: well, Kevern showed them how much they could get away with.

But by the time I could work out the words that adults said, I understood what shaky ground my life stood on. There had been portents, people whispered. There had been signs, even before my mother's labour began, so they said. I was a dreading and a hissing in the dark, and if it had not been the greatest crime against the Mother ever known, Kevern would have strangled me in the cradle.

But Kevern, at least, was an identifiable and constant menace and one that could be predicted: I learned to be silent, I tried for invisibility, and I found a kind of solace in training myself not to feel anything at all. Not the hurt from insults or japes at my expense, not the pain from kicks or shoves, not the hunger pangs when meals were withheld, or blame (and punishment) for others' misdeeds were laid at my door. I tried to be stone, a wall of granite - I believed in that like a sacred creed, because a rock feels nothing.

I heard the rumors and the whispers, though. Bad luck, they murmured, and made the warding signs openly, not caring who saw. Not a cow could sicken, nor a wine turn sour in the cask that was not ascribed to my silent presence, though most stopped short of calling me witchborn outright. Ill winds followed me, said old Badb, our healer, trying to soften the dislike that dogged my steps, little as he cared for my company himself.

As long as my grandfather lived, all this mostly stayed within certain bounds: Kevern was at least shrewd enough not to overstep when the current lord still had the option of designating another heir than his only daughter. There was his sister's son as well, a man grown and well-known as a warrior, and nothing in our land-deeds could have prevented this as a choice. The manor-folk took their cues from their lord, and tended mainly to ignore my existence.

My mother was a different kind of threat. She was wildly changeable: at times filled with lilting laughter and careless affection that could, without warning turn into blinding rage over a servant's clumsiness or a child's misstep. Sometimes she gave me kind words and sweets, then beat me for having sticky hands, after. She might ignore Kevern's treatment of me, she might distract him suddenly, allowing me to escape, or she might decide to join in: it was impossible to know just what could happen. She was beautiful and strange: I wanted desperately to believe the best in her, and so here the stoniness broke into a thousand grains of sand, and she trapped me, every time.

I don't remember quite what happened, that one day. She must have been in one of her happy moods, and then we were in the stony-walled little shrine underneath the main hall, and she was drawing out the patterns with a bit of white chalky stone. Her "acolytes" as she named them - a couple of serving girls with a touch of the Gift, I reckon - watched, half fearful and half excited, their lips whispering whatever chants she'd taught them. There was smoke, and something overly sweet and cloying in the air, and I was crouched in a corner, filled with an almost paralyzing sense of wrongness I could not name.

She beckoned to me. I remember feeling sick, and I think I shook my head - nothing could have made me enter the circle she had drawn. She called to me, softly, beguilingly, and a part of me desperately wanted to go, I wanted her to be pleased, but I could not.

I remember the sound of my own whimpers, the drumming of my heart, and the way her face changed as she stepped forward to take hold of me, and the scream of rage when I turned, squirmed and ran.

I don't know what might have happened. I have never known and I have never wanted to know. I had gotten as far as the first rack of bins in the storeroom between her shrine and the stairs, but she had me cornered there and was but three steps away when my grandfather arrived, grim and silent.

No one spoke. He walked calmly past her and held out his hand to me. I took it and we walked upstairs. The day resumed ordinary proportions: I sat beside old Badb the healer at the table and ate whatever scraps were doled out to me, I listened to one of the soldiers who had a strong tenor voice sing an old and familiar ballad, and then found a quiet corner and curled up in a ragged bit of blanket, closed my eyes and tried to forget everything.

Two months later, my grandfather was dead, felled by a bad cut that turned evil and poisoned him. My mother nursed him through three weeks of pus, pain and fever, indeed, would let no one else near him.

I was only a child, but I thought I could see the link, as clear as pure springwater. Being a child, an unwanted, unloved, cursed child, I assumed, for a long time, that the link was me, and that I had caused his death.

And even though that child recognized what a hell I lived once his mitigating influence was gone, it was still impossible for me to believe, in fact, what she had done. Even now, a tiny part of me hopes I wrong her, hopes she did not kill him simply because he would not allow her to do whatever it was she intended to do, that day below the stairs.

The changes came faster after this. The life I led got very much worse, with nothing to stop it and then, suddenly, about a year after Grandfather's death, it did stop, in a way.

My mother was pregnant. Everyone seemed delighted. And it meant, for some reason, that no attention was paid to me at all. I had been banished from the great hall at mealtimes before my grandfather's corpse had had time to cool, and now, although there was no kindness at all left in my life, and I had to more or less steal what food or clothing I needed, I felt something less than a target.

I wondered, though. Was it true, as people said, that I brought evil with me wherever I went? Accursed brat, they called me, when they called me anything at all, and nothing in my life had taught me otherwise. Would I curse my parents' good fortune, even now?

I was nearly eight. If I stayed out of sight, no one inquired after my whereabouts, and it might be days between any forms of torment - Kevern's attention was wholly on my mother and the expected babe. My days were spent out wandering in the woods or hanging about in shadowed corners, listening and watching and trying desperately to make sense of my world. Occasional slip-ups drew Kevern's attention and inevitable cruelty - there seems no other word for it - but I got better at creeping about unnoticed. The entire world I knew was preoccupied with the imminent birth, and no one had any time to waste on me, for good or ill.

And so Meryn arrived into love and plenty, and there was even less time or energy for hating me, it seemed. She was plump and happy, a gurgling bundle of adorable babyhood, and everyone instantly was enchanted.

You might think I would be jealous, and so as an adult I sometimes wonder that I was not, but her charms caught me, as well.

I had crept into her room late one night, to see this marvelous creature that everyone was so enthralled by. Her wetnurse was snoring beside her, but Meryn's eyes were open in the darkness. I saw them glitter, silvery-blue in the moonlight, and she smiled up at me, and I was undone.

It was as if she knew my every hurt, my every sin, and loved me still, and I - well, I was instantly hers, for life.

I was her older sister, and in my child's mind, I suddenly feared for Meryn, an overwhelming and intense, unreasoning fear that only the tormented can know.

Had the mood all been like that for my birth? No one said so, indeed, quite the reverse, but I already had observed how often people claimed to have had forebodings of doom after the fact. People like to believe they are wiser than they truly are.

I could imagine myself, looked for and wanted, and cosseted until something had happened to turn them all against me. No one ever spelled out quite why it was that I deserved to be so unloved, and my life had taught me only that adults were irrational and wayward, without any sense or logic to their likes and dislikes.

It could happen to her. Who was to say why or when? Who could predict what tiny infraction would cast her out into the wilderness I inhabited? What chancy moment had laid my fate on me? And because it had been a simple case of love at first sight, I was determined that she would not go unprotected. I watched over her, quietly, from the shadows, her silent and invisible champion, ready to sacrifice anything and anyone to defend her.

It never came to that, of course. Meryn went from strength to strength, her first tooth exclaimed over, her first steps delighted in, her first words repeated from one end of the hayfields to the other. She could do no wrong, in my eyes or anyone else's.

What did happen was marsh fever.

Chapter Five

Most years, there's no fever at all. Other years, a few people come down with it, and maybe they die but mostly not, and no one thinks overmuch on it. That year, when I was ten and Meryn just past her second naming day, it came with a vengeance. Old women used to tell of years like that, but it had been long and long since it had felled so many and so swiftly, long enough that even for those old crones it was a memory from their own grandmothers, told like fireside tales to scare the toddlers into being good.

Old Badb went early, along with three guards and a pair of serving girls, almost before anyone knew what was afoot, and by the time anyone realized that this was no ordinary marsh fever, half the servants were dead or dying, most everyone else was showing symptoms, and no one had the slightest idea what to do about it. It took the hardy and the hale almost easier than the aged or the weak: Kevern ordered the digging of a massive pit grave only hours before he, too, began to show signs of illness, and he did not linger. By sun-up the next day, he was dead.

My mother shut herself up in her room, hysterically demanding that no one come near her and then, just as hysterically, demanding food and wine. A few hours later, she was found crawling on the stairs, delirious and begging for water. There was almost no one left to hear her pleas.

It had gone suddenly from chaos to silence. No one, I realized, was looking after Meryn by then: any still-healthy folk had fled. I found some unsoured milk and day-old bread, and fed her and changed her filthy nappies. She seemed unfazed by the strangeness, playing quietly or sleeping, while I hovered over her anxiously, watching for any sign of the fever. In the morning, I slipped out into the silent halls, scavenging for a little food and water, stepping casually over the dead and a few nearly dead people I had once known, and making it back to Meryn's room, more preoccupied with what I should do if there was no food to be found on the morrow than with any thoughts of the horrors around me.

When the soldiers from Gorsedd came, we were the only ones left alive in the hall, and it had been the better part of two days since we'd eaten. I heard later that the outlying farms did not fare too badly, and quite a number of the villagers had survived, but here at the centre of the manor, there were only the two of us left to be saved.

It was late when we reached the castle at Gorsedd. I had heard tales - it is a high place with a long and honourable history, and a source of pride for my grandfather, to be allied with such an illustrious family. The relationship was tenuous; a collateral marriage some generations back, but it had been strengthened by overlapping fealties and mutual interests, and it seemed that the Lady of Gorsedd valued it as well. She was, I gathered, prepared to take us in, and see to our welfare till we were grown.

There was a fire burning in the hearth, and tall white candles set on the table. The Lady sat in a high-backed chair, the first one I'd ever seen, and her robe was deep red with a richly embroidered hem.

It seemed right to bow, although how I knew this is a mystery. No such ceremonies had ever come my way, but perhaps some bit of an old tale or song informed me. I set Meryn on her feet beside me and bobbed in what I hoped was the correct fashion. I had no idea what to expect - I had no reason to think that I would not be as reviled and loathed here as anywhere else, but if by my actions I could spare Meryn any pain or insult, I was prepared to accept whatever was given to me.

Meryn, having never encountered anything to fear in her life so far, smiled up at the Lady and trotted forward. Her eyes were on the heavy medallion that hung at the Lady's neck, symbol of her priestly office. She reached the Lady before I could catch her skirts to hold her back, and reached up to her, murmuring "Pretty toy", and I froze in terror.

"My Lady, she doesn't know -" I stammered.

But the Lady merely laughed, bending down to scoop Meryn into her arms and set her on her lap. Meryn clutched at the medallion and then put it into her mouth. I was very nearly sick.

"You have a liking for that, poppet? Well, the Goddess knows her own, certainly." And she smiled at me.

"My poor girl," she said. "You have had a dreadful time these last weeks. And how you must mourn your dear parents. But have no fears - you will find life here most congenial, I am sure. Indeed, my son is eager to make your acquaintance, since you are so close in age, and he pick up the necessary courtesies and behaviors anyway, but the Lady liked to coach us in the finer details. There was the added bonus of meeting and becoming friends with people who might well ease our way later in life: had my grandfather lived, or my parents given any sort of care or thought to my potential future, I might have ended up here anyway, to learn, and to grow under the tutelage of more well-heeled and well-connected nobility.

I saw less of Meryn than I would have liked. She had been swept up by Lady Ilona's personal attendants and borne away that first night, but the instant bond we had formed in her infancy had been strengthened over those strange days as the manor-folk died around us. She wept for me the second night, and would not be comforted till one of the women was sent to fetch me, and it became a regular ritual for me to visit her in the evening.

I was still a stone, a granite wall, where others were concerned: no teasing, no anger, no disgust could have touched my frozen heart, but when Meryn would run to me, shrieking with joy and throwing her chubby little arms around my neck, something deep inside me would break, just a little. It was a terrible weakness, I knew it, but despite that, I cherished it and would not willingly miss a moment in her company. She was the one true thing in my life, and I kept it locked up hard within me.

But as time went on, she began to have her own life, too. She was drawn naturally to the service of the Goddess, which was only to be expected in a place where the Lady ruled as priestess as well, yet there was more to it. Everyone remarked on it: she seemed born to the role, and there was talk of sending her, when she was older, to the holy isle for training.

"Not but what she won't get a better education here," Nesta pointed out. It was likely the truth. The Lady Ilona was famed everywhere for her knowledge and skill, there were those from Braide and other places, even as far away as Kerris, who sought her counsel on numerous occasions.

Still, there's prestige in training at Braide, and the Lady was adamant that Meryn should have every advantage.

Nesta herself was here as much for this sort of training as for the courtly graces she might pick up, and the more advanced sword drills weren't, originally, supposed to be a part of her life. That was Nesta's own choice, and she was glib enough to have talked her way around the Lady's initial objections.

Nesta was my first real friend, in a way, because she liked to tell me what adorable things Meryn might have said or done during the day, and I was always willing to listen to that. When I realized that we had progressed to discussing other topics, it was too late. I rather liked her: she was funny and opinionated and gossipy in a way that was curiously free of malice, and I wouldn't, I knew, willingly have done her harm.

I grew friendly with the others, too: Iain was good at bringing us together, which was lucky for me, and having named himself my cousin, he had given me a bit of standing.

Feargal really was his cousin, of course, he'd been orphaned young and had scarcely known any other home, he and Iain growing up like brothers. There was Baile from Carric, not the brightest boy but wholly good-hearted and well-meaning, there was Daire, who was the youngest son of a southern lord the Lady had trade connections with, and Elen, who was the best archer among us. She had a sour wit and was quick to take offense, you had to be careful with her.

You would think that over the years there, I would have gained some confidence. I was, within a twelve-month, acknowledged as the best fighter - even Cowell admitted that I was not altogether worthless on the field, and would, if I applied myself and did not succumb to arrogance, possibly make a decent warrior someday. If I was not the most congenial of companions, I was not considered a social outcast, either: if there was any plan or activity afoot, I was included as a natural and expected participant.

Nor was there ever, on the part of any adult, even the slightest suggestion that my education and keep at Gorsedd was less than my due, or in any way grudgingly bestowed. The Lady went out of her way to make me feel more than welcome, always. Indeed, she frequently singled me out with marks of favour, sometimes inviting me to dine with her in the little solar above the hall, asking for my thoughts on

He'd learned, even then, a fierce control. It was only by the tiniest movement of his shoulders that he even hinted at his relief that he had not had to ask outright.

"There's a little walled court by the old stables," he said. "No-one goes there, and the gate guards can't actually see into it from the wall. We could manage an hour at least, if we went while Tiernan's at Council."

I nodded. "I'll bring the gear. No one will even notice if I'm the one hauling a couple of swords around. Tomorrow, then?"

No one ever just practices. You have to talk about things, and then someone reaches for an analogy to illustrate their point, and the next thing you know, you are making your case on a point of honour, or the advantages of peregrines over goshawks, or why your grandmother swore by bean porridge on frosty mornings.

And there you are: privy to how someone's mind works and what they care about, and either you know that you will have to tread warily with them forever or you are fast friends. Sometimes, as with Einon and I, it was a bit of both.

Chapter Seven

There is a thing that happens, when people grow comfortable with their position in life. They take it as holy words that they are entitled to what they have. Along with everyone's tendency to see themselves as "the good ones", they give themselves additional justifications not only for keeping things as they are but then enlarging upon it and demanding more for themselves as their due.

Inevitably, tyranny reigns.

It is true enough that having wrested control of secular affairs from the priesthood - a hard-fought battle and one well worth fighting - that things were better for most people. Even itinerant labourers found it easier to make ends meet when the local priestess could no longer simply commandeer their bodies or their earthly goods on demand. Farmers could lay by stores for less plentiful times and the nobility certainly gained much by not having to submit every decision to the whims or scrutiny of the local servants of the Mother. The well-connected and the well-born amassed greater fortunes than ever before, while still keeping the holy ones' good will by not stinting on gifts and outward respect, and that was good for those below them, too.

From our line of sight, things had then gone badly wrong.

As the men and women who had seized control of Dungarrow grew older and secure in their victory, they had become hardened with it. They had promised fairness, and in a sense, they'd delivered, but "fairness" was now taken to mean the same tithes and fees for everyone, regardless of individual circumstances, and the difference of a one-twentieth share from a rich man and a poor one meant that in some years, even the lesser gentry suffered serious deprivation and hunger, while the well-to-do got fat on the proceeds.

Their crime was mostly age, as far as we, in our youthful arrogance, were concerned: age seemed to us to bring with it an inflexibility of mind as well as a miserly, self-centred stance where the men and women in power seemed bent on merely replacing the evil they had suffered with an evil that benefitted them instead.

We felt that we were different, and that we would remain so always.

We wanted a world where even the least among us could be free from outright devastation, and where exalted position came with some enforceable responsibilities. It seemed madness to drive people to the desperate, despairing edge, especially mad when the people doing this had once suffered from much the same condition.

Trevian, who was another one of Iain's cousins, the old lord of Gorsedd's sister-son and temporarily Iain's heir, should he not get another, well, he had some trenchant things to say about poverty and greed. His lands were under constant threat by his overlord, who considered Trevian's holdings as a back-up larder in lean years, and treated Trev as if he were still a toddler and addled into the bargain.

We of Gorsedd weren't the only ones, of course. Our little circle grew to include most of the younger folk who were brought in their parents' wake to the ducal court, and even a few older landholders and nobles, who had seen what unchecked greed was doing to us all, they, too, began to lend quiet, tacit support to the idea of change.

Yet until Einon articulated our rages and our dreams, it had been an incoherent, unspoken sense of wrongness. He laid out in no uncertain terms just what we meant by all this, what we faced, and how for some of us, it might tear our lives apart. We would have to break with the past, and in some cases, with people we loved. It was dangerous talk, dangerous talk that could lead to dangerous deeds, but for some of us, that was, perhaps, the appeal.

It was all just talk, at this point. Even so, over the years, Einon drew us together, bound by these values, but ultimately bound ever tighter by our love for him. He was curiously charismatic even at an early age. There was something about him that made you believe in impossibilities, and in your own best self, and it held us together even when outside forces would have predicted otherwise.

Those of Orleigh, for example, did not willingly spend time with those of Gorsedd, at least not without blood being shed. It was an ancient feud, but at this moment in time, it was at the simmering stage, not boiling point. And so Iain did not draw daggers when Guerin of Orleigh became part of the growing pack of admirers around Einon, and Guerin managed to rein in a natural bent towards sarcasm when he directed any comments to Gorsedd's heir. They were stiffly, scrupulously polite to each other, and tried desperately not to discuss the same issues, since they could not bear to be seen to either agree or to quarrel.

Beholden to Gorsedd as I was, I had to follow the same line, but Guerin, a little older than we were, was able to separate loyalties from personalities, and always treated me with a lazy kind of respect, as if he expected me to have thoughts of my own. He was right in this - I could see clearly that the old, clannish enmities were as much a problem for Dungarrow as the rapaciousness of the nobles - but I kept these thoughts to myself. Guerin had a mischievous streak that I distrusted. I wasn't ever secure enough to risk Iain's friendship for even the slightest sign of agreement with anything Orleigh might say, and waited to see where Einon's judgment lay before committing myself to anything aloud.

It might have gone on like that forever. At our age, it certainly seemed as if it would, since none of us had any real power - even Feargal only acquiesced, as I did, to the decisions about his property that Lady Ilona "advised".

I cared less about it than he did, but Penliath was not anywhere near as exalted or extensive as Feargal's holdings were. I shared it with Meryn, as well, and she needed me to make good decisions on her behalf. We, at least, were lucky in that Lady Ilona had found us an excellent steward. The woman came, twice yearly, to report soberly on the harvest or the year's shearings, while I fidgeted and agreed to whatever plans for the future she and Lady Ilona thought best.

Despite our taste for rebellious discussion, our live were normally placid. We changed so little and so slowly that I, at least, was unaware that time was passing faster than I knew.

To teach us our craft, we were sometimes taken along on springtime coastal patrols near Dungarrow Castle, to be parked in some out of the way place in the hills to watch as real soldiers swept the beaches clean of raiders. Before leaving us, the troop commander would read us dire lectures on remaining where we were, and reminding us that we were only there on sufferance and to observe the tactics of how fighting was when death was imminent. We came armed, but that, he sternly announced, was to get us into the habit of war. We were not heroes.

We were useless baggage he had been saddled with. He expected us to obey orders and stay put.

They were confident and self-assured, those warriors, secure in the experience of multiple seasons of success, and we shared that easy trust. We envied them, not quite grasping that battles are chancy affairs and that fate can turn on the tiniest of mis-steps, despite the frequent warnings from our teachers about the tides of war.

One blustery morning, though, as we sat on a hillock a half-mile above the beach, everything changed.

The troop had ridden down, as always, at good speed, swords out, against a ragtag little band of raiders, all Istaran by the look of it, who were just reaching the shore when it became apparent that someone had miscalculated badly.

Another, larger group of fighters emerged from a fold in the hills, well inland from their comrades just landing. A dozen or so of them broke off, running to attack our troopers from behind, while the bulk of the group began heading for the higher ground.

Heading, in fact, directly towards us.

It took a long moment for it to sink in. We stood, immobile and disbelieving, waiting for this to change, waiting for our troops to see and ride to our rescue, waiting for the unthinkable to vanish and for our untroubled world to return.

They were almost on us before years of training finally took hold.

I heard Einon yelling "Form *line!*" and someone bellowed "Swords up!" and then the world shifted forever as the raiders came up the hill.

They were laughing. I heard a hissing past my ear as Elen's first arrow took out one of them, yet they were laughing still as they closed in. A big one, black-bearded and swinging a heavy-looking axe, locked eyes with me.

There was no battle-joy, a thing I'd heard of from the bards when they sang of heroes. Cowell had spoken to us of that kind of madness - the bloodlust, he'd called it - it did no one much good, to hear him tell it. We'd been told not to let our ignorant excitement take us beyond caution, and people had warned us, too, of the fear that is an ordinary warrior's lot, and how we could not let it overpower us, but to use it, crafting it into an anger that could be sent into our sword-arms, to lend us strength.

No one had ever hinted to me that I might be bored, though.

It was as if the world had flattened, dampened down, and I was aware of a curious detachment, as if I were both there in fact, with my sword upraised, and then, as well, as if I were standing a little way off, judging someone else's performance on the practice ground.

I saw, as if the world had suddenly slowed, that he was going to swing the weapon high and to the right, and I dodged sideways to his left, slicing my blade into his ribs, but there was no time to see if I had felled him. A tough-looking, fair-haired woman was right behind him and I watched as my sword slid around and up and into her unprotected gut, as if it knew what to do without me. Part of me marked her look of affronted surprise as she went down, and then I turned instinctively to see another fighter advancing from my left.

He was younger than the others, maybe only a couple of years my senior, really, and he, at least, wasn't laughing anymore. He came at me warily, his shield up and his brow furrowed, and I thought he should be worried because I was still in that state of unnatural calm, save that now both my mind and my body knew what they were about and were weighing up the options. This was what I was meant to do, it was as easy as breathing, and I danced a little to his right and dropped my sword low.

It was my favourite trick on the practice ground, back then. You let the sword slip out of sight below the rim of your opponent's shield and wheel it back up between the two of you, turning the blade to angle above their head and letting the momentum of the drop provide the additional power as it chops to your opponent's neck. With practice it goes very fast, and I had had a lot of practice.

Easy-peasy. The blood gushed out, spraying me, my foe and Feargal, as well, who was not two feet away, just pulling his sword free from another of our attackers. I hadn't known before how much blood a person could have in them.

It was over then, as suddenly as it had begun.

Roisean, whose father held the ports at Fencair, was excitedly describing Einon's first fight. She'd been right behind him, bent on stepping in to protect him if need be, and was now unabashedly proud that his age and lack of inches had not hindered him at all. Guerin was calmly cleaning his sword, and Iain was guarding at swordpoint the one Istaran still alive.

I hadn't killed the first one. He had fallen to Einon, who had, according to Roisean, managed first to dispatch the band's leader by being much quicker and using a step-and-thrust move to duck under the man's range and gut him quite efficiently. Turning, he'd seen the man I'd slashed at starting to get up again, and killed him before the bastard could struggle to his feet.

For a moment, as we saw that we - two dozen untried adolescents who were now blooded warriors at last - had vanquished our opponents, we were noisily exultant. We had proven ourselves. We were children no longer.

Slowly, though, a silence fell over us. Elen stood uncaring and still, as blood dripped from a shallow cut on her arm, and reality began to chill us in the warm spring air.

Baile…he lay unmoving in the sand. Part of his face was gone, and a strange part of me was transfixed, noting every detail, as if some important question lay in his wounds, one that could be answered and understood.

The troop captain had left the dead and dying on the beach and was riding hell for leather to us, but the damage was done. Elen was weeping openly, and we had all of us, even Roisean, grown very quietly grim. He could take his time, I thought, and tried to wipe some of the blood from my face.

There was, in the end, nothing we could say or do, nothing that could change things. The older troopers gave us rough praise and curt advice, the younger ones commiserated and warned us gently that this, too, was how our lives would be from now on, and gradually, the shock of it wore away and we felt only sadness.

Or so the others said. I stayed silent, because in the end, I realized once more my essential difference from them.

I felt nothing at all. Oh, I had liked Baile well enough. He had been funny and kind to animals and a little unwise in his speech, and I could see, in a remote sort of way, that things might a bit less amusing without him, but no tears came, no sense of regret or loss or sorrow touched me. I felt only a certain cold satisfaction that my attackers had not bested me and that, in the eyes of the world, I was a warrior in truth.

Chapter Eight

I never gave much thought to my appearance when I was young.

In the beginning, it was at least partly because no one cared whether I was clean or dirty, or taught me to care for this. At Gorsedd, I saw immediately that combed hair, regular washing and clean-ish clothes were important, and imitated the others, but focused as I was on simply fitting in, the implication that these things had more importance than just being like everyone else escaped me.

The first hints I had that I might be, on some level, likable in another way that had no relationship to me as a person, came in the few weeks leading up to my Goddess Night.

It's likely the same, deep down, for every girl, no matter how pretty or plain she might be. Even quite old men felt free to comment on our approaching womanhood and the delights in store, although if they were very much older, it was considered crass and unmannerly to do this to our faces. The younger men, the boys we'd grown up with, they could be quite crude, but that became a more muted chorus after Nesta bloodied Daire's nose when he detailed a rather imaginative scenario involving himself, Nesta, and a horse trough full of water.

I don't know why it is that only girls have to be subjected to this. The boys saw it simply as their Goddess-given opportunity to get that one experience older men brag about, not but that a few of them hadn't found a willing partner to lie with already. But there wasn't the singling out, the marking out of any of them as less than men, once they'd been blooded in battle. Only we girls had this: one, last, publicly commented-on humiliation to be endured, before the world would accept us as fully adult.

The priestess who instructed us told us repeatedly that daughters were sacred. Daughters were the roots of the world, and precious to the Mother of All. When we had questions, her only answer was that this night was a Holy Mystery and that it was given only to us, the Goddess' special and beloved daughters, to help us understand and to bear what life would bring.

It didn't seem much of a gift. It felt like an unwelcome ordeal, to be honest, and I could not, for the life of me, see the point of it. But then,

I had not even the tiniest belief in a Mother who looked out for Her children, although I could well imagine Her in Her more fearful and judgmental aspect as the Destroyer of Worlds.

They made us bathe in a sacred pool, which, as it was fed by streams of melting snow tumbling out of the mountains, was incredibly cold, even in high summer. We loosed our braids and twined flower garlands in our hair. We dressed in the long, white, sleeveless shifts that symbolized our state of transition and the Lady Ilona had made sure that the girls in her care, like me, were clad in the finest-woven bleached linen, so soft and delicately thin that we might easily have been naked.

We were walked in solemn procession to the sacred grove, the priests and priestesses repeating once more the things they'd been drilling into us for weeks: to run free, to embrace the wildness within us, and to accept with gladness whatever the Goddess willed. Then the Reverend Mother, who had come over from Braide as a special courtesy to the ducal court, kissed each of us tenderly, blessed us with the ritual words, and they all departed.

There was food and sweet wines laid out for us on the grassy space in front of the shrine, and a few musicians were hidden among the trees, playing merry tunes as we drank and feasted our way out of girlhood. Out beyond the sacred grove, we knew, there were any number of young men, quite a few older ones, and probably some women, hoping they could run fast enough to catch the girl they wanted.

Holy words said that the Goddess chose for us. Holy words said that try as a man or woman might, only She determined the outcome. Holy words said that the Goddess gave us this night as a harbinger and a promise, for our lives hereafter. A gift of prescience, if one could read it aright.

There came a point where the music's tempo subtly altered and it seemed as if everyone except for me felt things change, a movement of the spirit. They began to get up, to link arms and dance around the stone offering slab and then, one by one, to spin off into the woods around us. I knew instinctively that to be the last, to not at least appear to feel the Goddess-good that moved the other girls, was to be different, apart, and I could not afford that. I had been watchful, and I timed my behavior to be firmly among the middle lot - not too eager, not too much behindhand, just an ordinary girl with ordinary desires and ordinary hopes for the future.

Out in the forest, I could hear laughter and shrieks of merriment. We had been instructed to run, to make the boys chase us, and most of the girls were enjoying this as much as the boys were. There was enough moonlight to prevent all but the most unlucky of accidents, and these were hills and woods we knew well. It still seemed rather oddly innocent and a bit like a game.

So I ran. At some point, I thought at least one man chased me. I thought I knew who it was, too, and that thought was almost immediately followed by "Oh, please, not him" and I scrambled up a little rocky cleft and doubled back, sprinting further up into the hills. He did not follow, and it occurred to me that probably, he'd been after someone else, anyway.

At another point, I almost stepped on a girl I didn't know, locked in furious embrace with one of the musicians who'd been providing our background entertainment earlier. They seemed neither to see or hear me and I ran on, until I tripped over a tree root and ripped my linen shift, and sat for a long moment thinking how stupid and pointless this entire affair was. No one appeared for me, no one gave chase, and I was stumbling around in the trees waiting - for what? For some idiot to carelessly have me, and then brag of it to his friends later?

It was tiring. I circled back, still hearing the echoing of laughter, although that was fading, too, as each girl paired off, and eventually, worn and depressed, I found myself back at the sacred grove.

Well, they had said the Goddess sent you a message about your life to come, what kind of life you could expect. If She spoke true through Her servants, then Her message to me was clear.

I could expect nothing in this life, nor in the hereafter.

I was of no account to Her, and, I decided, She was of no account to me. She could Be or not - it made no difference. I must find what I could in life, on my own and on my own terms. I picked up a handful of little cakes made from crushed hazelnuts and honey, filled a cup to the brim with wine, sat down defiantly on the offering stone and took a long, gulping drink to wash away the sourness of reality.

It was only after several minutes that I became aware that I was not alone.

He was standing at the edge of the clearing, as pale as stone in the moonlight, and as unmoving, watching me. The wine-cup slipped from my hand, and I felt, as if from very far off, the cold of the spilled wine soaking into my shift.

Guerin walked slowly across the clearing, his eyes on mine, till he stood not a hand's breadth away. We never spoke; his hands drifted up to my shoulders and he slid the shift down, away from my neck and further, and I stood, unbidden, and let the cloth slip uselessly to the ground.

And then something unknown took hold of me and the Goddess' power swept over both of us, spiraling wide and enveloping us into it and I felt, I believed, I knew, for one all too brief moment, that She was true, that I was loved, and that the world belonged as much to me as any other living thing.

I woke alone, in a cold dawn, on the offering stone, with only my stained, torn shift puddled on the ground to tell me I had not dreamed it all.

Not Feargal: his wealth and connections protected him. A few soft words, a repentant apology, and a year or two staying quietly on his lands, and it was entirely likely that Mael would let it lie, at least for a few years. Not Nesta, either: she'd married an older Baron whose position and large number of followers made him well-nigh unassailable. He was utterly in love with Nesta, and though he perhaps favoured Mael's candidacy himself, he was not prepared to lose her: whatever came, she'd be safe enough. Guerin, well, again, he had a father whose reputation and strong sword arm would keep his heir from any serious repercussions. It was a rare day when anyone would bet against the lords of Orleigh. My cousin Iain, too, was at no serious risk, I was certain. Lady Ilona was still a force to be reckoned with, and because of that, I also knew Meryn would be safe, no matter what came to me.

Indeed, when you thought about it, only a few of us were risking anything much. They all of them had families who would ward them, or else they were negligible enough that they could run off home and lie low till even Mael forgot just who was where on the fateful day. When you considered most of the likely outcomes, only Einon and I were risking death outright.

It had been the unspoken script beneath any plans we made. The old man couldn't last forever and so, for the last year or more, we'd been watching and weighing, determining just who it was that would be our strongest, most likely adversary. We had, without quite putting it into words, determined our strategy, and I, as the most expendable person in the group, was at the heart of it.

Ullien died around dawn, in the dreary not-quite-spring when the snows are gone, but the air still holds its chill.

The court's mood was now even more nervous and unstable; it had been long and long since anyone else had ruled here, and the future had never seemed so uncertain. And yet, there was an undercurrent of excitement, too, a sense that change might not be all bad. Some of those landowners and gentry who had seemed to be sympathetic to our cause were fading away, frightened that they might incur Mael's wrath or just hoping to pick up a few crumbs in the expected aftermath, but a surprising number of heretofore undeclared nobles began hinting that they, too, would prefer a less heavy-handed, might-begets-right direction for the dukedom.

The Council was called for the morning after the old man's pyre burned down, and in the two days between the death and the burning, it was as if the whole world held its breath. Even Mael was quiet - he was not a complete fool, after all, and could see the value to avoiding any quarrel or disturbance that might offend the Holy Ones as they conducted the rituals. No leader fights on two fronts if they can help it.

We came down the stairs, a full warband, ready and armed, though only one of us would fight. The nervousness was palpable, but I didn't care. My mind was on Mael.

We had to stop this before it started. We couldn't let him get as far as the Council chamber, where our youth would lose us the battle before it began. The reality was that only three of us yet held our own lands outright and could be granted the right to speak, and we would be forever outmatched by those with years of experience in finessing the decisions there. It had to be out here in the open courtyard, it had to be a legal challenge, and it had to be final. There was no other way.

I'd been watching him for months, surreptitiously studying him as he sparred with his friends and supporters on the Dungarrow practice ground. He fought as all big men tend to fight: he used his reach to keep the fight where he wanted it, and he relied on his weight to push people around on the field. Most of his friends were the same, but they tended to concede the tactics and let him dictate the terms. They concentrated more on not being too easily beaten than on neutralizing Mael's appropriated advantages.

It's common enough. People are trained, in a way, to fall into agreement with the loudest voice in the hall.

But while I wasn't the smallest person to ever take up the sword, I wasn't usually the biggest on the field, either. I had had to learn a different way, not of fighting itself, but of how to approach any match with the ability to change and adapt and take control away from that loudest voice. I was used to changing the rules. And while it would have been unwise to spar directly with the man himself, I had managed a couple of good sessions with some of the fighters who most resembled him in size and style. I always made a point of losing to them, as a precaution in case they ever mentioned the fight to Mael.

I knew, by the time the rituals for the beloved dead were taking place, that he wasn't anything like invincible. I knew what tricks he was likely to use, and I had a fair idea of what his back-up strategy would be when those initial ploys failed him. I knew, in fact, that I likely could beat him, if I was willing to pay the price.

The greatest of the land were already at the gate and one could see at a glance which way they thought this wind would blow. They were clustered around Mael like hens around the feed basket.

"Whatever you do," Guerin said to me as we headed down the stairs towards the doors out into the courtyard, "Make it quick. We can't let them have time to think."

It was easy for him to say. He only had to stand and watch.

"Welcome to Dungarrow…cousin."

Einon had pitched his voice low and calm, easily heard and utterly dismissive. The pause itself dripped with insult.

It worked like a charm. Mael might well have been expecting at least a token challenge to his ascension, but something as blatant as this was a spark to tinder for his friends. They bristled like dogs on the scent.

"The bantling cock crows loudest before the slaughterhouse door," Mael said derisively, and of all the responses we had anticipated, this one was on the mild side. We'd hoped for something more. Still, it was close enough to work with.

"Do you deny my claim?" asked Einon, his voice still even. "Do you dispute my right?"

"Indeed I do. Children have no rights: they do as their elders bid, and I bid you go play with your toys and leave the business of rulership to your betters."

This was much better. No one could expect Einon to let words like those go too easily. I flexed the fingers of my sword hand, itching for this part to be over and done with.

Einon raised his eyebrows and said, almost sorrowfully, "Is that a challenge to me, Lord Mael?"

"Take it however you like."

"Fair enough. Will you fight for it here and now, or will you turn tail and run?"

There was a gasp and then a swirl of muffled, nervous laughter. You could understand it. Einon stood at least a full head shorter than Mael, still bony-thin in his boyhood. It must have seemed like suicide.

"Aye, I'll claim this once and for all…boy."

And then, just as we'd rehearsed it, I stepped forward and said clearly, "Lord Einon, I claim right of Champion."

More suppressed mirth, and some open grins from those clustered closest around Mael. The mirth didn't reach the people further out. This wasn't an auspicious way to start a serious Council.

"Too scared to fight your own battles, boy?"

"It is his right," said someone near the back of the crowd. Thank the Goddess we hadn't had to raise this point ourselves, and in actual fact, it was only Einon's right if he were confirmed as duke in law as well as blood. But Mael merely laughed.

"What's the difference between one babe and another?" he said, contemptuously, and it was in his eyes as they met mine, that he would kill me and then Einon, and take pleasure in it, too.

I looked away quickly. I was afraid of only one thing now, and that was that I make him doubt his obvious superiority too soon. Half a duel's outcome hangs on what your opponent thinks will happen before it starts.

I walked out into the open space before us and drew my sword. I was ready for anything, including Mael not waiting for the witnesses to declare themselves and the ritual words to be said to make it a legal challenge, but he was in no hurry. He shrugged out of his cloak and handed it off, took up his shield, and drew his blade.

proceedings. All my thoughts were on staying upright and not causing a fuss.

I came back from half-consciousness to the slam of the chamber door and I sighed and relaxed and slid down the wall to sit, uncaring, on the tiled floor. Later I heard from Nesta that I left a terrifying streak of red, all down the fresh white plaster. Suddenly, there was a rise of panicked voices.

"She's hurt!"

"She's bleeding!"

I wanted to point out that this hardly mattered. We'd done it. Einon was duke. Part of me was obscenely triumphant, but mostly I just wanted to sleep. Someone tried to give me wine, but I couldn't make my fingers curl around the cup, and I started to laugh, then stopped. It rather hurt.

I'd known I was cut. I didn't think it was too bad. I tried to say so, but this seemed to frighten them even more, so I gave up and just smiled happily at Einon, who looked gratifyingly upset.

After a bit, a healer came. He was not impressed with me, my wound or my friends' attempts to make me drink.

He pushed away my tunic and my shirt, and examined the cut. I knew, as soon as I looked that I had been right. It wasn't so bad. It was the bleeding that had made me lightheaded and sleepy.

"You need to get her to her chamber. She needs rest, and plenty of it."

"No," I said, as forcefully as I could.

"Yes" said the healer, firmly.

"No," I said again. "Tonight. The banquet. I've got to be seen. No show of weakness."

Einon frowned.

"She's right," said Guerin. "If word leaked out…"

Some people might think it had been a fluke. Some people might decide, on reflection, that Einon's position was not as strong as it had seemed that morning, that anyone might have the dukedom for the asking.

Some people would, eventually, but we needed some time. We needed time to bind enough of the nobility to us that we could withstand what was coming.

I needed to be seen, hale and hearty, in the great hall that night. It wasn't up for debate.

The healer, of course, did debate it. He warned that I risked a fever or worse, and that I was courting disaster, which was pretty funny considering the morning I'd had.

In the end, though, he did as his duke bid him. He cleaned the wound, sewed the cut closed, and wrapped the bandaging flat against my side with no unsightly padding, so that in a clean tunic, nothing would show. He insisted I rest until the last possible moment before I entered the feasthall, and admonished Finon to prevent me from drinking.

"I must," I said. "I must drink his health, at least."

"Mind the wine's well-watered, then, and don't blame me if you are in a high fever by sun-up." He was still grumbling under his breath as he left.

Chapter Ten

Looking back after, it was a good year, that first one. Hard, of course, since we weren't mistaken about a fair number of the nobles and even some of the gentry thinking that the changes Einon stood for threatened their eminent positions as well as their purses. We were continuously under arms almost from the very start, but there was a certain enjoyment as we surmounted the obstacles, one by one.

Lord Siubhan was no sooner back on his lands before rumors drifted north that he was plotting. We'd expected it, to be honest. He'd always been close to Mael, of course, and even at that first banquet, watching him toasting Einon, it was obvious to everyone that his loyalty wasn't even skin deep. Days later, he was home and whispering poison and promises into other men's ears.

If anyone doubted my right to my place as Einon's champion, I earned it many times over in the first few months. Many an older warrior looked me up and down and decided a challenge was less risky than open war, since Einon had managed to win support from a great many people. Killing me was seen as an easy way to power.

Siubhan went for war, instead, thinking we were just young fools drunk on our victory and all unready for outright rebellion. Not a full month after I'd killed Mael, we met Siubhan's band of discontented friends and vassals in the hills above Boirand, and the first spear was cast.

He was no tactician. He led his troops headlong towards us, with nothing left in reserve, and if he'd listened to his scouts, it didn't show. Lord Fincair had sent two troops of battle-hardened warriors to be captained by Roisean and we'd stationed them in a copse less than a half-mile away, while Einon proceeded to lure Suibhan's forces into the dales that lay to the west. When we finally engaged them outright, Roisean led out her troops and attacked their flank, folding them neatly into their own lines, and the thing was nearly over when Siubhan decided to cut and run.

He'd little enough support left, but it would do no good to let him get away. Mischief comes in all sizes - even without his lands and money, he might still do harm. Einon ordered me out with the newly-formed ducal guard, to make sure the man didn't survive another day.

I killed a lot of people that year. Siubhan was easy: he'd learned his game from Mael, but not nearly so well, and he'd seen me kill. Defeat was in his eyes even as our swords first met, and I wasted no time with him.

But even as he lay dying, the holy ones woke up to the fact that an untried boy who still technically should have had a Lord Warder ruling in his stead represented their best chance to drag us back to the way life had been fifty years before. We went from Boirand to Dungarrow Castle on a forced march at a breakneck pace to find it the victim of a hastily organized siege, which we broke in a bloody battle that cost both sides dearly.

Einon then barricaded the principal river landings and himself led the delegation to negotiate with the Reverend Mother, pointing out that the island she lived on depended on regular shipments of food and other goods to survive. Einon's regretful musing that constant war might interrupt those shipments seemed to make his point more forcefully than any show of arms had done, and the Reverend Mother made sure the priesthood understood where their loyalties now lay.

Over time, the idea that Einon wasn't strong enough to rule died away, as it became apparent that, boy or not, he was a brilliant general in the field and not at all averse to advice, whether he actually took it or not. He wooed enough of the older nobles onto his side by at least pretending to listen to them, by never losing his temper, and by being realistic enough to not try to change everything overnight.

There were those, though, that were simply going to be dangerous to the realm, no matter which way the winds blew, and Einon needed them neutralized before they could start trouble. It was my duty to pick quarrels with them and force a duel to remove the potential threat

Tiernan was one of those, although, petty as it seemed, Einon wanted him gone for more than the simpleminded treason he was engaged in. Those years on the practice ground still rankled, and I had no objection to killing the man, if it would ease Einon's mind.

It was a hard-fought bout. Tiernan was no Mael, he was wary from the start and kept his defense high. I had to offer the bait of my shield arm to get him to lose that canniness and follow a fake to his head before he went down, and it was months before I got my full strength back. Even now, that shoulder sometimes pains me in wet weather.

Ullien had never named a permanent champion, preferring to give the nod to this fighter or that on the rare occasions when he needed to seem above the fray. Otherwise, well, he'd been a man grown by the time he wrested control from the Reverend Mother who had acted as Warder after his aunt died, and it had meant a lot to him to fight his own fights.

For Einon it was different. Even later, when he gained his full height and filled out, becoming the equal of any warrior in the field, he preferred to leave the lesser battles to me. It allowed him some leeway, after, and he accrued less of the blame, allowing people to come to the conclusion that the new ways weren't so very bad, after all, and to pretend to loyalty until that loyalty became their own in truth.

But because of that, because the role of ducal champion had become by the second year, a permanent thing, and one of prestige and curious honour, it began to be contested on its own.

It was seen that Einon trusted me, and that despite Penliath's relative unimportance, my opinion carried weight with him, both in and out of the council chambers. I sat close to him at table, I accompanied him almost everywhere, and when he was exhausted or irritable, I was the wall between Einon and the rest of the world, ensuring he was not troubled by annoying sycophants looking for favours.

Some people, especially those who hadn't been in the courtyard at Dungarrow that day, took one look at me and decided I'd just been lucky and that an open challenge was an easy road to fame and fortune.

And so I had battles to fight simply for myself, and the place I occupied. There were always young fighters, and even some older ones, eager to earn their reputation by killing me, and it's easy enough to throw some points of honour around to force things to a head.

Usually, I brushed through these brawls without a scratch, because most people have a wildly over-inflated estimation of their own abilities, and they weren't very often anything near the warrior they thought themselves.

Once or twice, some petty lordling would attempt an ambush instead, thinking that a couple of hired bravos on a deserted stretch of road could do the job.

I didn't always come through those unscathed, but I came through, nonetheless.

My boredom in battle increased. Every experience made the next one that much easier, every bout taught me more about how others fought. The rest of it became a game for me: watching and listening and being able to predict who would be my next opponent, and Feargal and I started making hilarious bets about the who, how and when.

We'd always been friends of sorts, Feargal and I, even from the start. He'd been the only one to never mock me about my lack of swordsmanship when I'd first stepped onto the practice ground, and his inheritance made him generous, never having had to think twice about where the money was to be found. He liked the people around him to be happy, and if he thought some trinket or some adventure would do the trick, he arranged its existence in your life in some way that could not be argued with or resented.

Our friendship grew stronger, because we were devoted to Einon back when almost everyone else was sorrowfully rationalizing why being close to the boy was not worth the risk. In the first year, the long evenings sitting in the hall outside the ducal bedchamber, drinking and dicing and waiting for the slightest suggestion that our presence might be needed, those nights only reinforced and strengthened our bond.

We became a bit of a team, and occasionally, as the need for constant attendance on the young duke's pleasure lessened, we wound up in Feargal's rooms, making love in a companionable sort of way. It was part of our friendship, and to be honest, neither one of us was ever touched by the slightest of heart-aches or even any serious desire for the other. It was just an entertaining way to pass the time when nothing better was on offer.

I was just back from Emlyn Glais, where I'd been at pains to negotiate with a band of minor gentry who resented a proposed tax on mill-rights. Outnumbered, they had decided to fight, as if it wasn't two years on and we didn't have a string of hard-won victories behind us. An arrow had glanced off someone's shield and into my sword arm - the wound wasn't deep, but it felt achy and bruised, and had made me irritable. Einon had at first been sympathetic, then frustrated with my grunting responses to his questions about the battle, and finally he ordered Feargal to take me away and get me drunk.

It wasn't so much a marriage proposal as a business arrangement. I wasn't rich, and my position in Einon's court was not easy to maintain, in terms of suitable clothing, weapons, horses and so on. I hadn't the aptitude, or even the time to spend overseeing Penliath, and the income there had to be split with Merryn, anyway.

Einon, it seemed, was concerned that I would be distracted by these mundane problems. He wanted a solution that ensured my financial position while costing him nothing.

The trouble was two-fold: Ullien, despite appearances, had not been such a good steward of his lands as we had all assumed, and his use of bribery to bolster any flagging loyalties had depleted things further. Einon had far less ready cash or future income to work with than he'd imagined he would have.

In addition, he was concerned with appearances.

He had to be. Asking all those lords and ladies to give up even some of their rapacious ways and let those lower down the ladder become more prosperous wouldn't look quite so fair if he then handed someone as lowly as Penliath's holder some appropriated spoils that made me rich. I'd had a few small gifts, such as a very finely-made mail shirt and a new horse, as well as a pair of farms that abutted Penliath, but those had been in dispute as to ownership since my grandfather had been a lad, and no one regarded them as ill-gotten gains.

More than that might seem like hypocrisy. In fact, I had been the one to point it out to him, when he'd suggested I take over Mael's acres of grazing lands, a few weeks after the duel in the courtyard. Disinheriting his vanquished opponent's two sons wasn't a good way to win friends, either, and I had argued for generosity there. I didn't need any new reasons to watch Einon's back or my own.

But Feargal laid out a solution that he claimed would benefit us both. He was under pressure from his many cousins to marry, since his position demanded direct and attested blood- heirs whenever possible, and he was damned sure that marrying anyone who might reasonably expect a claim on his affections would be the road to unhappiness.

Better a friend he trusted, he said, than some clingy girl with dreams of fidelity and heart-to-heart hearthside chats about grain storage or pig farming. Better a strong sword arm at his side, he said, and as to heirs, well, we were young yet. If I was willing, in a few years, to give up the time to it, he'd be grateful. If not, his relatives would have to lump it.

The clincher was, of course, that Einon approved of it. Nay, he had suggested it. What could be more reassuring for him than two of his closest friends united by the strongest of ties? Nothing need change, Feargal said. We'd just go on as we were, but he could, through generous bride-gifts, make sure that neither Merryn nor I need want for anything, ever.

And in among those gifts, along with some excellent jewels, a lucrative river crossing and three large grain fields complete with a mill, were the fealties, fees and messuages of the Vale of Rhwyn.

Chapter Eleven

In the end, Eardith and I ate our fish supper alone, frying up two of the trout over the fire as Guerin and Arlais rode on for richer fare and warmer beds up at Rhwyn Keep.

Arlais had spent a fruitless hour, questioning me about the wolves, but Eardith had spoken truly in her letters and there was little I could add. I saw why they'd sent Arlais out from Braide, though.

Young as she was, she appeared to have a profound and encompassing knowledge of ancient and arcane lore: nothing I said seemed to surprise her. She took it all in with equanimity, exchanging knowing glances and occasional nods of comprehension with Eardith, and while I built up the hearth fire and got out the iron griddle, Guerin saddled their horses and she and Eardith stood on the grassy verge of the path and held a worried, low-voiced conversation.

But once we'd cleared away the dishes, and set the last trout in a pot of water to simmer for tomorrow's porridge, Eardith said,

"She'll want to go up into the mountains, you know."

"She's welcome to the journey."

But her tone alerted me. I sat back down on the bench and waited.

"Well, she can't go alone," Eardith said, her voice pitched sweetly reasonable. "And Joss is far too busy, this time of year. I doubt Owain can spare him."

I was trapped. I didn't even bother to rack my brains to come up with an excuse, and just muttered that I wasn't keen on this.

"Nonsense," she said. "There have been no more wolves - you and Joss managed things well enough. But she feels she must see the place."

I caught the uncertainty beneath her cheery tone. She didn't like this either. Our eyes met.

"Oh, I'll come as well," she said, finally, unwillingly, I thought. "But you'll be perfectly safe."

"Really? Almost a whole day given for a moment's worth of a look-see? You must be far more observant than I, to gather so much out of so little."

"Caoimhe. Leave it," said Eardith sharply.

"No," I said. "No. You dragged me up here. I want to know what happened. I want to know how three wolf carcasses can just disappear without a trace. I want to know why three children died to no purpose. If there are answers here, I want them."

"You won't find them poking around here," she said, "and you wouldn't understand the answers if you had them, anyway. But we would do better to be home before dark - I promise you, this place is not one that you should linger in."

"Oh, I'll grant you all of that and more," I said, drily. "But you are the one throwing magic about like poultry feed. I'd like some kind of explanation. Hells, I'd settle for a decent lie."

She flinched.

"Caoimhe," said Arlais, and now there was just the slightest thread of urgency in her voice, "We will tell all we can. But not here. Not now. Please."

I looked at Guerin, who shrugged.

"Whatever they will say can be said as easily in Rhwyn as here," he said, after a moment. "And, truthfully, are you so eager to stay?"

I shook my head. It occurred to me that any explanation they gave me would be incomplete or false, whether they had had the leisure to think it over and match their stories, or had to blurt things out all unprepared. And while many people think that having time to concoct a tale means they will give less away, they are almost always wrong. Well-constructed stories and justifications are mostly the product of people being over-clever and outthinking themselves. Given enough time, they will try to fill every possible gap, explain away the troublesome details, and focus your attention on the things they consider safe.

It's truly revealing, what someone else thinks is important enough to deflect you away from.

Chapter Twelve

I should have known that any promises made would not be kept.

Oh, I don't say Eardith hadn't intended to tell me some things, and I expect that some of those things might even have been true. But if life had taught me anything these last twenty-two years, it was that chance interposes itself between the promise and the fulfillment, and that things almost never turn out the way one expects.

And so, while a pitched battle on Rhwyn's village green was not something I would ever have predicted, when I look back, I think I did assume that some kind of reality would throw us off course.

We'd heard the sounds of it as we rounded the long sweep down from the crossroads, and Guerin and I had exchanged one look and dug our heels into our horses' flanks. As we came over the hill, what we saw was utter pandemonium.

When I say a pitched battle, I mean it. There were well over a hundred armed fighters, they were at it hammer and tongs, and it was as inexplicable as the sun in a rainstorm. In the first moment, I could not have said who was fighting who, but then I saw the dark blue ribands trailing from some of the helms, and I knew, at least a little bit, who I needed to kill.

We came down at a gallop, swords out and to be honest, there was no one I'd have rather had at my side just then than Guerin of Orleigh. The years of fighting the same battles, often side by side, meant that we both knew, instinctively, what we needed to do. There was no fear that either of us would do the wrong things and there was the utter trust that the shared experience of countless war-fields brings. We needed no words, we needed no thought. We simply reacted, as long experience and training kicked in.

I had feelings, though, of a sort. One was that I was absolutely the last Goddess-be-damned thing those Camrhyssi needed right now, because I was already in a bloody bad mood. Killing was going to feel quite good.

Balefire shared this sentiment, apparently. He was tense and trembling as we hit that first hard shock of battle engaged, snorting and snapping and kicking out at the first fighter who turned towards me. I hardly had time to swing my sword before the man went down, screaming in pain.

The next in line had his shield up high. I leaned low and sideways over Balefire's neck and smashed him in the side of his face with my sword pommel and then my horse's hooves did the rest. But this was not the best move, from my standpoint. I was out of practice and Balefire had reared back before I'd had time to rebalance. I rolled off his back, hitting the ground with a force that winded me. Not a good place to be.

Something threw a bulky shadow over the fighter bearing down on me, and suddenly, the soldier advancing fell, bleeding, and there was someone reaching down from his perch on the saddle, hauling me to my feet.

"Idiot," said Guerin, cheerfully. "You owe me a pint of ale."

All around, the sounds of battle were fading. The furious shouting and the loud clash of sword on sword was slowly replaced by the groans of the wounded and dying, and the barked commands to form up, to go for healers, to guard those prisoners.

I looked around. Rhwyn was victorious, but they owed nothing to our late arrival. We'd been some salt poured onto the wounds, that was all. The outcome had apparently not been in any serious doubt.

There had been the dozen or so of Owain's household guards, ill-trained part-timers all, struggling against fifty or so well-armed Camrhyssi. I had no idea what they were doing there, any of them. Camrhyssi raiders had never bothered a little place like Rhwyn before.

But beside those guards who made up Rhwyn's fighting forces, there was also a strong contingent of troops flying the colours of the royal House of Machyll, and that made no sense at all.

Dungarrow is part of Keraine, it's true. But not in any way that truly matters: the kings and queens who occupied the ornate thrones in the city of Kerris seldom asked anything of us, and certainly not anything that might disturb the traders sneaking over the border to sell cloth or buy grain. It was a given that Dungarrow had no interest in antagonizing Camrhys to any point that might send sizable forces over the few passes still open in the north. We had enough work with

Istaran raiders, feuding clans and homegrown bandits - we didn't need an overtly hostile army on our doorstep as well.

And so the rulers of Keraine accepted a limited, qualified form of fealty from the dukes of Dungarrow and asked only that we not allow Camrhyssi raiders to claw permanent footholds on this side of the mountains. That was easy enough, since the Camrhyssi were as dependent on the clandestine trading and a reasonable image of peace as we were. Both sides behaved, in essence, as if Dungarrow did not exist.

So why a king of Keraine had troops this far north, and why the Camrhyssi had elected for open battle just here, just now, was unfathomable, and more than a little worrisome.

I was still absorbing their unlikely presence when I turned to see a man of Gorsedd, a man I knew, bending over to put a whimpering horse out of its misery.

What, in the name of Aheris, was Cowell doing here?

***

In the end, I rode back down to the cottage alone, filled with unanswered questions and serious misgivings. Owain had offered me a bed, but I could see that Rhwyn Keep was descending fast into chaos and that his wife would not thank me for becoming yet another headache in her already fraught and unfinished day.

In addition to these many soldiers out of the south, she had been further burdened, all unprepared, with the presence of Birais, King of Keraine and inexplicably, the Lady of Gorsedd. It was an open question as to which of those two guests terrified her more.

The Camrhyssi were easily explained by Birais' presence, in fact: he'd been chasing them all the way from a pass north of Glaice, because instead of surrendering and waiting to be exchanged for a few minor trade concessions or some decent ransom, which was the usual drill, they'd decided to run for it.

The Lady's presence was harder to fathom, though. Oh, her words made sense, after a fashion, and in the press of the crowd in the courtyard, I hadn't thought overmuch on it.

Now, watching the embers of a dying fire in the cottage's hearth, and listening only to the evening breeze and some energetic crickets, it made a lot less sense.

***

My marriage had followed closely on the heels of another: Lady Ilona had brokered a hugely advantageous match for her son to a southern lord's only daughter, and that wedding party had come north with great fanfare, just as soon as the harvest was brought in.

The festivities quite eclipsed my own, which was a relief. I couldn't have borne that kind of scrutiny or the public comment that attended their nuptials. People remarked openly on the bride's beauty, which was considerable, but also, more quietly, on her stiffly haughty manners. The charitable might put it down to shyness, but glimpsing her occasional secret, sardonic smiles, her coldness towards those of us closest to Iain and her behavior towards her new husband's servants, I could see that she considered us all very much beneath her. Even her father, Lord Uln, seemed to find Dungarrow and Gorsedd lacking in sophistication and refinement, and could not resist some smilingly sarcastic comments. Iain, I surmised, wasn't destined for a pleasant married life.

He went south with her the following spring, and when he returned that fall, he came alone. She was already pregnant, and the local healer had advised against travel. It might have only been me and my eternally cynical mind, but Iain seemed rather relieved to be home, and threw himself back into life at Dungarrow with enthusiasm.

***

That Lady Ilona had chosen to accompany Iain back south, this time for good, apparently, and to visit her daughter-by-marriage and her grandson this spring was a thoroughly reasonable explanation of why she had been in the south. Attaching herself to a royal war party on the hunt for a large force of Camrhyssi invaders, though, was more of a puzzle. She'd have been sooner home sticking to the main roads, and far safer as well. And there had been something odd, something both eager and repressed, in her bearing.

She had almost immediately been in close conversation with both Eardith and Arlais, and I was surprised to realize that she knew them both well. Eardith the more so, obviously: they had, the pair of them, been students at Braide together, long ago. They all three retired to Ilona's room, and I was left, standing uselessly about in that sea of soldiers, horses and baggage, until Cowell had come over with a message from Eardith saying that she'd be remaining here for the night.

That was the point where I looked around, saw Owain's wife struggling to organize this unexpected domestic disaster into something that might allow for reasonable mealtimes and beds for everyone, and politely went over and explained that Balefire wasn't at all happy about the crowds and I would take him home and out of her hair, if she didn't mind.

Now, in the darkness, I turned the day's events over in my mind, and wondered just what in all the Nine Hells was going on.

Arlais, well, she knew something was up, and she had some understanding of it, but I had sensed she was only just beginning to grasp at what it might be. Her obvious relief at seeing the Lady of Gorsedd, another someone older and infinitely wiser to whom she could dump the more urgent part of this mess onto, well, I completely understood that. But she at least could probably put some words to this, and I most certainly could not.

That Eardith held the key seemed certain. She had known, I realized, before ever we left that morning, what it was that was there. Indeed, not even the disasters with the wolves had seemed to surprise her. Distressed and dismayed - certainly she had been all of that. Worried, too, and as eager as anyone to find a solution. But surprised - no, she hadn't been anything near that.

In point of fact, now that I considered it, she had been expecting it. Perhaps not the wolves, not specifically, but she'd been bracing for something, and for a long time now, too.

Chapter Thirteen

In the morning, Balefire being still restive and a little fractious after the previous day's exertions, I let him out into the open meadow beyond the garden and walked up to the manor on my own.

I'd dreamt of Meryn in the night. I sometimes had before, although I rarely remembered the substance of it, just waking with the feeling of having seen her, or the sound of her laughter echoing in my mind.

This time, though, it had been quite vivid and more of it stayed with me. I could almost feel her hand on my arm even now, insistent, urgent. She'd been trying to tell me something, but there was a roaring in my ears, like a winter storm screaming through the trees, and all I'd caught was her crying out my name.

It had woken me before dawn. I'd lain there, full waking and dry-eyed, and with a chill no fire or blanket could ease, until there was light enough to see by and I could reasonably tell myself that it was only a dream, after all.

Lady Delwen had done as well as she could, given Rhwyn's limitations. Every possible space had been pressed into service, and while some of the king's soldiers had had to be housed in an unused cow-byre, the courtyard was clear of horse-droppings and excess gear, and she'd had an awning set up near the gatehouse, where several troopers now lounged, drinking, dicing or repairing their kit.

The hall was still more crowded than I'd ever seen it, though, even during festival times. They had set up a table at the farther end of the room, and there the king sat, with a few of his closer retainers. Lord Owain was there, too, looking nervous, and, unsurprisingly, Guerin was there as well, leaning idly back on his bench, paring an apple with his eating knife and looking wholly at ease. He saw me as I was weaving my way through the knots of strangers infesting the space, and he waved, not in welcome, but in warning.

I slowed my pace, wondering what it was that might put me in peril, but before I could even begin to consider this, there was a tug at my sleeve.

"Arlais?" I said, surprised. "I'd have thought you'd be with Eardith and the Lady."

"Those two..." her voice was tense and I could see she was upset, upset and angry, and not hiding it well.

"I need some air," she said, after a moment. "Walk with me. Please."

We started back down the hall towards the door. Arlais was setting a frantic pace, shoving at anyone who blocked her path. Being as pretty as she was, and wearing the marks of a priestess, no one hindered her, although they were certainly annoyed by it. If I had tried that, there would certainly have been a bit of a barney, but no ordinary soldier or household servant willingly takes a priestess of the Mother to task for poor manners.

She left me in her dust, therefore, as I eased my way around the people she had simply pushed past, quirking my eyebrows up or shrugging my shoulders in sympathy, as the case warranted, and tried to keep up.

We had reached the open air, but Arlais kept moving, bent, it seemed, on putting some distance between herself and anyone else. At last, when we'd gotten past the gates and out onto the road, her steps slowed and I caught up to her.

She'd begun to pace back and forth along the road's edge, kicking at the occasional stone in her path. I waited. If she could walk off some of that anger, I might even get some sense out of her.

"Those two," she burst out, finally, stopping a few feet away. "You would think I was some green little mooncalf, instead of -" but then she broke off, drew a long breath and said, more quietly, "I am *not* an ignorant child."

I could have had more sympathy, I suppose. I did have some - I knew how I'd felt, before that day with Mael, when older people dismissed my very existence as negligible and of little account. But the truth was, I thought, that to Ilona and Eardith, Arlais *was* a child, and surely, in terms of experience, she had little enough she could have put up against them. In any case, I had concerns of my own here.

"Arlais," I said, "Out there, in the mountains. What was it that happened?"

She sighed. "That's the point, isn't it? There is something evil in that place. We all felt it, did we not?"

"What do they say about it?"

"It is what they do not say," Arlais said, savagely. "Well, and what sort of fool do they take me for, telling me it is just an old aura, clinging to the rocks? I know a present danger when I touch it, whatever they might believe."

She might have said more. She was prepared, even eager to say more, I would have sworn it, but then her gaze slid past me and her lips tightened. I turned to see Eardith heading toward us from the gate.

"Arlais," Eardith said. "Arlais, we should talk."

She didn't look well. There were dark shadows beneath her eyes, and she was leaning heavily on her walking stick.

"Talk? Talk is all we've done these last twelve glasses. It might be more to the point if you were to actually say something."

I did have to admire Arlais. She had some courage, and a fine touch with sarcasm. It would have been funny, if yesterday had never happened.

"It is not something to scream from the rooftops," Eardith said, gently enough. "Look you, this is not the time or place. Mayhap if we -"

We were, I realized, doomed to interruptions today. One of Owain's servants had arrived, unnoticed and a little out of breath.

"Please, my ladies. The lord is asking for you." I could have punched him.

The household servants were laying out a morning repast. It wasn't anything fit for a king, of course, just bread and cheese, with a platter of the scavenged bits of last night's roasted chickens for the more exalted folk at the table, but they had rolled in a cask of ale, as well, and no one seemed discontented.

I saw that Lady Ilona had joined the group at the table. She had a wine cup in front of her and she was listening intently to whatever it was that Birais was saying. They all were like that, hanging on his every statement like it was holy words. It might have been anything from trade policy to reminiscing about a boar hunt, I couldn't tell. I was merely glad none of it would include me. Courtly conversation is almost always duller than ditchwater.

Lady Delwen caught up to me as I filled a mug from the cask.

I complimented her on the arrangements she'd managed. Ilona had schooled me well in the courtesies, and I had not forgotten her hints that people liked to have their accomplishments noted.

She looked pleased, but harassed.

"The king," she said, nervously. "The king, and the Lady, too, I don't know what they think. It's always the same, when she comes. I wish people would send word."

I frowned. I couldn't think why Ilona should ever have come here before, but then I remembered this valley had belonged to Feargal. There might be a reason there, although, given Rhwyn's lack of importance and the carelessness with which he'd given it away, this seemed tenuous, at best. But before I could ask, Delwen remembered why she had sought me out.

"You'll stay tonight? The banquet..." here she paused and made a wry face, "such as it is. The king. and Lady Ilona, too, they were asking after you."

It confused her a little, I could see. For three years, I had been just a bit of rubbish tossed up from a springtime storm. Rubbish that was occasionally useful, when some trader's guards laughed at her husband's makeshift household troopers and Rhwyn could count on me to give the lord's commands some actual teeth, or when a little extra brawn was needed in the fields.

Why the rubbish should now be invited to sup with a king was a question that disordered her world, but she wasn't one to look at things too deeply. She was merely relieved when I nodded. Her attention was immediately distracted by one of the scullery boys dropping an armload of wooden platters, and she was off again, taking her worries back to the kitchens and the linen-presses.

I didn't envy her. Truthfully, it takes less skill to kill things than to care for them.

I had hoped that I could slide unnoticed through all this. I had made my courtesies to Ilona the night before, bowed in the king's general direction on cue and then told Guerin where I would be, and it had seemed then that interest in my existence and my whereabouts was blissfully minimal. Now, however, one of the king's men, a rather young one, was heading towards me.

I glanced around for Eardith and Arlais, in the hope that I was not the primary object here, but they were nowhere to be seen. The man sketched the tiniest of bows, muttered a surly request that seemed more bereft of actual words than was customary, and gestured at the table.

"Lady Caoimhe," Birais said, nodding at me as I came up. "Will you join us?"

I bowed. I walked to the end of the table, where Guerin was moving over to give me room. It was just courtesy, that was all, I thought. Just the courtesy of a man who was known for his good manners to his underlings, that led me here.

The talk resumed - it was as I'd thought. They'd been rehashing yesterday's battle and now had got onto the most prized qualities in a warhorse. I let the talk wash over me, having little to contribute, but I became unnerved by the occasional glances Birais kept flicking my way, as if he were on the point of asking me a direct question, yet curiously unwilling to do so outright.

His young henchman, too, kept his gaze on me. He'd taken up a post at the side, leaning against the wall with his arms defiantly folded, every inch the truculent warrior barely leashing in his emotions.

He might, I realized, know who I was. Anyone might have told him. Lady Ilona? Guerin? Not Eardith, I was sure, as she wasn't one to give even the tiniest mite of knowledge away without some purpose, and certainly not to a stranger, not without some good reason.

But if the king's man knew who and what I had once been, then I knew what his angry eyes meant. He was calculating the odds and working out the when and where.

For the maximum glory, it would, of course, need to be in a formal setting, and in full view of as many folk as possible. If he killed me in any other way, there would always be questions, there would always be doubters. If you are going to kill a renowned killer, you want the full measure of credit, or what's the point?

The old, familiar boredom deadened my spirit. It would be this evening, I guessed, once the tables were laid, and he most likely had some spurious excuse ready to hand. There would be some foster-friend or distant relative that I had killed, I reckoned.

Really, it was only too likely that I had. The nobles both north and south had married and fostered into so many of each other's families over the centuries that the true wonder would have been finding someone who couldn't use this as an excuse to challenge me.

He wasn't so much bigger than I was, but he had a sturdier build, and something about his stance told me he was used to getting his way, on and off the field. Spoiled and headstrong, I reckoned, sizing him up, and he hadn't yet met anything in this world he couldn't bluster or bludgeon away.

I'd met his kind before. I'd killed his kind before, too.

Chapter Fourteen

I've endured longer days, I suppose. Idiotic behavior comes in many guises, but an impromptu king's visit to a backwater village might well be the worst. There was all that subtle jostling for position, for one thing, not just from Birais' own troops, but from a couple of Owain's people who saw a chance at prestige and advancement. One seemed bent on being noticed by Birais himself, another was currying favour from one of the royal troop captains, and yet another was, slightly more realistically, trying to convince Cowell that she would make an excellent addition to Lady Ilona's entourage.

Birais retired to his room in the afternoon, on the spurious excuse that he needed to consult with his captains regarding the disposition of the few Camrhyssi prisoners they were holding, and Lady Ilona once more swept Eardith and the obviously unwilling Arlais up and disappeared with them into the little walled kitchen-garden.

Left to our own devices, Guerin and I wandered down to the stables. His mount had come down with the colic that morning and after an emetic draught, needed constant walking. With so many extra horses, though, it was certain that this was low on the stable-hands' list of priorities.

"That soldier of Birais'," I said, as we led Shadow down the road towards the village, "the one watching me…"

"Aye, he seems a bit on edge."

I glanced at him. "Does he know who I am?"

"Caoimhe," Guerin said, gently. "Everyone knows who you are. Even when they don't know, they know."

"What in the Nine Hells does that even mean?" I said, exasperated. I don't know why it was that nearly every time I talked to Guerin, I almost immediately lost my temper.

"You are who you are. You are what you are. People talk, you know."

I waited. Usually, if you wait, most people will tell you something else, just to fill the silence.

Guerin wasn't most people. He smiled amiably and began whistling.

I said, "He's going to challenge me, you know. Probably tonight."

The whistling broke off.

"Ye-es. Yes, he probably will."

"Why? Why should he do this? What can he gain? It isn't as if I am still Einon's champion."

"Oh, that," said Guerin, almost apologetically. "Well, that might have been partly my fault."

I waited again. This time, for once, he swallowed the bait.

"The thing is, someone was talking about you. And he said he'd heard it was a fine thing, being Dungarrow's champion, and he'd a mind to it. And I pointed out that the last time someone voiced that thought, Einon said that as far as he knew, the position was still filled."

"And how," I asked, trying to keep my tone disinterested and even, "how, in the name of Aheris, does Einon know I am even alive?"

"I should think Owain wrote to him almost immediately, don't you?"

My estimation of Owain rose several notches. He'd never even dropped the slightest hint. Well done, Owain. And it explained Guerin's presence here, too, I thought, with an uncharacteristic sense of something like optimism. Acting as escort to a priestess on a fact-finding tour had struck me from the first as an unlikely errand for Guerin of Orleigh.

"So, what happens next?"

Guerin stopped. A moment later, I did too, and turned to look at him. He wasn't smiling.

"Caoimhe, as far as you're concerned, I have no instructions, invitations or suggestions of any kind. Nor messages either, although Einon did seem to want to know if you were still… all right, you know."

I felt it then, a faint sinking of the heart. It was the tone of Guerin's voice, I think. Almost as if he were trying to be kind.

You would have thought I was immune to anything like hope or its cousins, wouldn't you? I had certainly thought so. I reminded myself that I was not a living thing. It could not matter. It must not matter. Be a rock.

Shadow snorted. Guerin reached up, patting his neck and murmuring soothing words, and began to walk on, and after a moment, I did as well.

Over the course of the afternoon, I tried to find out more about my possible opponent. It wasn't easy. I didn't know most of these men and women, and they had better things to do with their time than talk to me, anyway. In the end, I sought out Cowell, although I didn't expect much to come of it.

He surprised me, though. Last night, he'd greeted me formally, almost as if I'd been the merest acquaintance, and I hadn't expected more. An oath-breaking murderer is not someone people care to be seen as friends with, after all.

But today, running him to earth out by the kennels, he grinned, punched me in the shoulder and said I looked well enough.

And he knew who I was asking about. Apparently, he thought that I did as well, although for the life of me I could not remember the boy at all. He was some sort of relation to Birais, and he'd visited Dungarrow with his father about a year before the old duke had died.

His name was Lannach.

"He's one to steer clear of, or so I've heard."

"I don't often get the choice," I said. "And I don't think he intends to give me one."

Cowell said, "Well, then. Young cock, crowing all the time. He fights like old Fencair's uncle used to do, you remember? All blows, no niceties. He might try a rush, thinking he can knock you down. And watch for the over-the-head feint. He relies on those. Used 'em twice in battle yesterday, and bragged about it. Thinks it makes him look crafty."

By early evening, the manor folk had set up all the trestle tables there were in Rhwyn manor, as well as borrowing two smaller ones from the inn, and improvising a few more out of scraps of wood and hastily pegged together carpenter's horses. Lady Delwen had, moreover, managed to commandeer every bench in the village, by the simple expedient of making it clear that everyone was welcome. No one would be slighted or left out. The villagers might get less meat and more broth down at their end, but they would be there. They could say forever after that they had feasted with a king.

Chapter Fifteen

They put me, not at the king's table, but at a seat at the table closest to the right of it, with Arlais and Guerin. Both were preoccupied with their own thoughts and did not seem disposed to talk to me, which was just as well. I was trying to think of some way to avoid what was coming, and not being terribly successful.

You might think, since killing people was the single thing I was good at, and having been a highly successful ducal champion, that I would go looking for fights. There are people like that, I know. People for whom killing is the sole point.

Me, I have never cared, either way. If ordered to kill, I did so. I trusted that Einon knew what he was doing, and that the killing was necessary. If I felt no pity for those deaths, I took no particular pleasure in them, either.

If I could find some way to prevent Lannach from issuing a challenge at all, I would take it. If nothing else, I didn't think the king was going to be very impressed by Owain's hospitality if he saw his kinsman killed before his very eyes.

I started scanning the crowd, looking for Lannach. The hall was full to bursting, though, and if he was there, I couldn't see him.

Birais came in, at last, with his captains, followed by Eardith and Lady Ilona. The Lady was finely dressed, as always; she must have travelled with a full string of pack ponies, and I wondered again, briefly, how she'd managed to keep up with a war-band at full gallop. There was the sound of scraping benches as everyone rose and waited, and then the disorderly noises that a crowd makes when sitting down again.

Then, just as they quieted, I heard his voice behind me.

"You're in my seat."

I very nearly laughed. Of all the boneheaded challenges, this one took the torch.

I turned and looked up and said politely, "I'm sorry. I didn't quite catch...?"

"I said, you're a jumped-up commoner, taking my seat."

"Ah." I smiled pleasantly and said, "Well, I am sure it was a simple mistake."

"Didn't you hear me, slut? You're in the wrong place."

"I beg your pardon," I said, mildly. "Please, do sit down."

Before I could move out from the bench, though, Guerin said lazily, "And here I thought the court of Keraine was famed for its especially good manners and gentle speech."

I have said I took no special pleasure in killing. At that moment, though, I could quite cheerfully have slit Guerin's throat.

Lannach, with his own desires already fixed, wanted no part of Guerin, fortunately. He ignored this jab and said, aggressively,

"Is this sniveling guttersnipe what the Duke of Dungarrow calls a champion? The only thing that could be more insulting would be to sit down with such a coward as had you to guard his name."

Oh, to the Nine Hells with this, I thought. I hadn't killed a hundred better than him in my time to let him publicly insult Einon to get what he wanted.

The hall had gone utterly silent.

I stood.

"My lord king," I said, and I used the carrying voice that Einon had taught me, the voice and words I'd used a hundred times before, "My lord king, I call a challenge."

"No!" said Arlais, in panicked tones. She grabbed my arm. I shook it off.

"If that is your will," Birais said. His expression was completely blank and his tone was studiously neutral. It occurred to me that Lannach was probably the kind of boy to do this a lot. Birais must be used to it. Used to the challenges and used to watching Lannach kill for no purpose.

"I call witness for Caoimhe of Penlaith, champion of Dungarrow," said Guerin.

One of Lannach's friends called witness for him. I reached under the table to where I'd stashed my sword. Someone brought me a shield.

"You can't do this," Arlais said. "You can't! This is madness. Lord Guerin, tell her!"

It was clear she didn't understand. The thing was done. Neither one of us could back down now.

"You need to stop this!"

I looked at Guerin.

"Try not to kill him," he said, cheerfully. "Einon doesn't need any difficulties with the king, just now."

I smiled, not very nicely. "That'll be fun."

"You're both mad," Arlais said. She sat down, picked up her wine cup with a shaking hand, and drank deeply.

I would have told her she was wasting her concern. That I wasn't worth the worrying and that Lannach, on the unlikely chance he did kill me, would be doing all of us a favour. But there wasn't any time for it. He had walked out to the space in front of the high table, and he already had his shield up and his sword out, all tensed and ready, and vibrating like a plucked harp string.

Oh, laddie, I thought, you're not just an ordinary fool, are you? You're the biggest kind of fool of all.

I sauntered out into the open space to face him, sword and shield hanging loosely at my sides.

Someone called the invocation. Lannach peered at me over the rim of his shield, and seemed confused by the fact that my shield and sword were still held carelessly at rest, with no semblance of defense.

Let's have credit where it's due. He wanted it to be a serious win, and he was willing to sacrifice something for it. He narrowed his eyes and waited.

"Are you ready?" he asked, finally.

"Aye."

He began to step in to throw a blow, but when I didn't move, he stopped it and dropped back a pace.

"Look you," he said, low-voiced, just as if he was on a practice ground, ready to teach some youngling a lesson, "You're supposed to - I mean...I will kill you, you know."

"Aye," I said, wearily. "Get on with it, then."

He re-set into that tight stance, frowning a little, and stepped a little to my left. I stayed put.

And then, all of a sudden, he threw himself into the thing, with a stride forward and his sword swinging over his head in the most obvious attempt at misdirection I had ever seen. I wheeled my shield up, blocked the actual shot and let loose a flurry of blows against his shield, knocking both the rim of it into his teeth and his whole body back as he retreated.

I went with him a few steps, still raining hard, deliberate hits onto his shield, and then let him fall back.

He was not a quick study.

He tucked back into that tight stance of his and came after me again, still opening with that same overhead fake, and I slammed my shield into his, then sent several more sharp blows against it, until he pushed away and backed up, breathing heavily and sucking at the blood on his lip.

I stepped away again, turning my back as if I simply could not be bothered, which was very close to the truth.

His fury was a palpable thing, now, a vast incoherence of rage, and I didn't even need to look. I felt him begin to move, and turned back.

It's all a matter of experience, speed and distance. Your opponent needs to be completely committed, and to have built up enough momentum so they cannot possibly stop in time.

He was less than two strides away, when I half-stepped right and leaned my whole body sideways, except for my left leg, still squarely in his path.

I didn't have to see his eyes to sense his last-minute, panicked comprehension, as he tripped over my foot. I swung my shield edge around and punched it hard into the back of his thigh as he fell, to make sure he went sprawling into a clumsy heap onto the floor, and I heard his sword skittering away off under one of the nearer tables.

He was winded, just for a grain or so. I walked over and knelt beside him, leaning down so that no one else could hear my words.

"If you aren't an utter fool," I said softly, "you'll let this end here. If you want to go on breathing, you'll take my hand, stand up, bow to me and to your king, and play the honourable warrior. Otherwise," I paused, "I can kill you now, of course."

He looked at me, no hatred nor anger left, only that ultimate, final terror. For all their vaunted trust in the Mother of All, most people are so desperate to go on breathing just that one moment longer, they'd sell their own grannies for another grain of the glass.

"Well? Do you want to live?"

"Aye," he whispered. "Aye."

I rose and waited. He rolled over and onto his knees, and I put out my hand. He grasped it and I hauled him up. We turned to the high table, and bowed, and, not wanting to push it further, I walked calmly back to my seat.

Chapter Sixteen

Arlais stared at me, constantly and with a kind of shock, all through the rest of the evening meal. I supposed that, despite my reputation and my explanation, she had not quite understood what it was to be Dungarrow's champion after all, and why should she have? No one goes a-dueling much on the holy isle.

Guerin had greeted me with a grin, a clap on the shoulder and a full wine-cup, and asked me where I'd learned that particular little maneuver. A few of the folk around us, troopers out of Keraine, mostly, congratulated me and continued to make sure my cup stayed full. Lannach wasn't well-loved, which was no surprise, and they had enjoyed the scene all the more because I'd let him live.

By the time they'd all settled down again and the boiled meats were being served, I had relaxed into that kind of unguarded tipsiness I rarely allowed myself. All's right with the world, drink and be merry, and hail-fellow-well-met: you know the sort of mood, I'm sure.

Then, for some reason, I glanced up at the king's table. Birais was looking at me with something like speculation, an expression that vanished as he caught my gaze. It was replaced immediately by that impenetrable mask again, but he raised his wine cup and lifted it towards me and then drank, and looked away.

That sobered me somewhat. When people in power look at you that way, they are almost always calculating what they might use you for, and so, later, I wasn't really all that surprised somehow, when he came out of the shadows as Guerin and I were making our way back to the hall after a visit to the latrines.

I bowed - it's a reflex, really, and good manners, Lady Ilona had always said, never hurt. Guerin attempted to do the same, but then burped loudly, grinned foolishly, and subsided to lean against the wall.

"You surprise me, Lady Caoimhe," Birais said, after a moment. "I had not heard that you were strong on mercy, yet, tonight, you chose not to kill."

I shrugged.

"Can I ask why?"

"Well, for one thing, no one asked me to."

"Ah. Do you only kill on command?"

"It depends on who is commanding," I said, carefully. "And... other things. Why? Did you want him dead?"

"Would you have killed him if I had asked?"

I considered this. "No, probably not."

"Then why...?"

"It's always interesting," I said, "to know another's thoughts on this. But would you have asked?"

"No," he echoed my own words. "Probably not."

He nodded then, as if he'd satisfied something in himself, and turned away, back to the hall. And then he stopped, and turned back.

"I knew your mother, a little," he said, and his voice was curiously flat. "A long time ago." He paused. "You are not much like her," he said, finally.

And this time, he did go, without a backward glance.

"That," said Guerin, "was...odd."

He sounded remarkably sober, and he wasn't using the wall as a desperately required support anymore.

"Yes," I said. It was odd, and unsettling, and I thought that I wouldn't rest easy until Birais took his royal self and his royal troops back south again. Being of interest to the king of Keraine was pretty much the last thing I needed.

All I wanted, just then, was to be away from here. I wanted it to be quiet, I wanted it to be ordinary, I wanted it to be as it had been for so long, before the wolves, before this unending stream of visitors to Rhwyn, and before the certain knowledge that my friendship with Einon was ended. I had known it was over, of course, known it the moment Feargal lay dead at my feet, but there had always been an illusion, a pretense that somehow, I still had something to return to.

Be a rock, I thought. Be a rock, be a wall of stone. Be no living thing.

"I'm for home," I said. Delwen had wanted me for the banquet, but she hadn't said anything about a bed for the night, and the heat and the noise of the crowded hall had lost any appeal.

"I'd offer you space in my chamber for the night," Guerin said. "But there isn't any. I've got one of the troop captains and his second in there with me. The second snores. Badly."

"No matter. I left Balefire in the pasture. He'll need to be seen to."

I retrieved my sword from under the table, and buckled it on, before it occurred to me that I ought, in all courtesy, relieve Delwen of any concern over me. I looked around the hall. People had been moving about, with Owain now sitting farther down the hall, talking to Joss, and Guerin was at the high table now, joking about with one of the king's men.

Delwen wasn't anywhere to be seen, but as I searched I saw Eardith, standing off to the side of the hall, watching Lady Ilona with an almost feverish intensity.

I began to watch, too. The Lady sat beside Birais and seemed to be asking serious, probing questions. She looked as if she was deeply interested and absorbed in the answers, yet there was something just ever so slightly off in the way she held herself, though I couldn't find any words that quite described it.

I couldn't hear the questions or the answers, of course. But something in me sensed that neither what she asked nor what the king answered was of even the tiniest interest to her. He could have been reciting nursery tales, for all she cared. It was as if she was trying to distract him in some way, for some obscure purpose.

I looked back at Eardith. She was very still.

I remembered how she had been, yesterday, in the mountains. Her hands and lips hadn't been at rest then, but there was something about her now that seemed the same.

I felt suddenly queasy, and I didn't think it was from the wine.

The holy ones, the ones with great talents, well, you hear stories. There had always been the suspicion that Braide's grip on Dungarrow had not only been because they were canny and wise and had taken advantage of temporary weaknesses. There were hints that they didn't always stay strictly in bounds in their quest for power.

I had, for most of my life, considered Lady Ilona my savior. Almost everything that had been good in my life seemed to have come to me through her, and the later losses had been my own choice; I couldn't fault her treatment of me. She had been like a mother to Meryn and I both, and even now, after everything, she had remained my friend. Even now, she behaved towards me as she always had, as if the last years had never been.

I owed her. And I owed Eardith, too.

I'm imagining this, I thought. I must be.

What I might have done, I don't know. At the very moment that the idea of somehow interrupting this, somehow disturbing Lady Ilona, or Eardith or even the king, began to take shape in my mind, Eardith suddenly turned and looked at me, and then produced a thin, rueful smile. A moment later, she grasped her walking stick and began to head down the hall towards me.

"You look exhausted," she said, by way of greeting. "Look you, I must get back home. There are things I need to see to. You should take to my room here, and get some rest."

I felt, as I had for so much of my life, as if I inhabited two places, two bodies at once. I listened to her far-off voice as she told me what chamber they'd given her. I heard myself tell her that Balefire had been in the field below the garden all day, and asking nicely if she could make sure he was well-watered before stabling him.

And all the while, I was still back in that other moment, still reliving what I had seen, trying to make sense of it, to see if there was some other, more sensible explanation that would fit.

Chapter Seventeen

Either out of sheer boredom, or because he had the sense to see the strain his little army was putting on Rhwyn's limited resources, Birais announced to the hall at breakfast that he intended to hunt.

This produced a flurry of activity. Arlais and the Lady were still abed, I gathered, and Eardith had not reappeared, nor Lannach, either, which was a relief. There's nothing so risky as a man who's had time to work up a new grievance to stitch onto an old one. Since it seemed an outing for the king's party, mostly, and I had nothing much else to do, I merely sat and watched as Owain gave orders to find enough spears for everyone, and the kitchen servants tried to assemble enough left-over food from last night to pack up as noon-day rations for the ones who were going.

But when I ventured out into the courtyard, I discovered I had been invited along on this, after all. Balefire was there, saddled and ready, and whoever had brought him up from the cottage had brought my hunting spears as well.

I wasn't sorry. While I didn't particularly want to spend a day anywhere near the king, I needed something to keep my mind from endlessly turning over last night's events, and I thought, in a party of this size, I could probably stay out of Birais' notice for a few hours.

Maybe.

It was the usual sort of excursion. People made the usual sorts of jokes, and there were, as always, a few false trails that came to nothing save some wild riding and a few caustic remarks.

But in the open country above the crossroads, the king found some sport, taking two white-tailed bucks, and it put him in a high good humor. When we stopped for a rest and some food while Joss organized the minimal butchering needed before transporting the carcasses back to the manor, I could hear Birais laughing at some jest from one of his captains.

They would leave on the morrow, I had heard, and probably Ilona as well. And then, when things were quieter, mayhap I'd get some sense out of Arlais. Even Eardith might tell me somewhat, although that was less likely. But sooner or later, all this would get sorted, Arlais and Guerin would head back to Dungarrow and their own lives, and Rhwyn would go back to being the sleepy village it had always been.

And then, I thought absently, I had best give some thought to my own future, such as it was. I still could lose myself somewhere. I could still take passage to Fendrais: Dungarrow wasn't the only port where the eastern merchant ships put in. Orleigh, perhaps. Guerin would know what traders were likely to stop there, and when.

The sun was making me sleepy. Through half-closed eyes, I saw that someone was coming towards me. For a moment, I assumed it was Guerin. He had been waylaid by the captain sharing his room and wound up on the grass over with the king's party, leaving me to my own devices.

It was Birais, himself, though, I realized. What on earth...? I straightened up and began to push away from the tree trunk that I'd used as a back rest.

"Nay, stay put," he said, waving me back. He sat as well, facing me.

"Tell me," he said. "Last night, you said it depended on who gave the orders, if you would kill."

"Aye."

"But...depending on what, is what I wonder."

"How much honour they have. How much trust I can place in them. And why they place their trust in me."

"Just their judgment, in the end? You just choose them and allow them to choose the rest? Do you never make those choices for yourself?"

"Once," I said. "Once, I did. As you well know, my lord, I'm sure."

And look how well that turned out, I thought.

He was looking at me with an expression I could not read. Maybe it was pity, maybe it was something else, I couldn't tell.

"How old are you?" That one caught me off guard. There was no conceivable circumstance where that could matter to him.

"Twenty-two, last Midwinter."

For a moment, he had an expression on his face that I couldn't put a name to. For a moment, I thought he was about to say something more. But then his face closed down so suddenly, it was like someone had snuffed out a candle.

"Ah," he said. "Ah."

He stood. He manufactured a smile and muttered a platitude about youth and wisdom, and just as suddenly as he'd come, he was gone, back to his friends and his captains, back to being the King of Keraine.

The sooner tomorrow comes, I thought, the sooner you are on your way south again, my lord, the better for all of us.

Although, come to think about it, there was no clear reason why I should have cared.

***

I visited Penliath only once in all those years after the marsh fever had come and gone.

It was late winter, and we'd been called away south to Davgenny over some banditry that turned out to be a local landholder trying to weaken another one, with the aim of taking over some lands she wanted. It was the kind of thing that Ullien had always turned a blind eye to if it involved a friend of his as the aggressor, or if he got a decent bribe out of it afterwards, and I suppose she hadn't quite taken in the fact that times had changed.

She played all innocence and tried to throw the blame on her troop captain, but then, in the darkness, she'd also gone for an assassination attempt and slipped into Einon's room with daggers drawn.

And met me, instead, because we never, in those early months, ever took Einon's safety for granted.

Still, she was good with a knife, and desperation lent her strength. I got a cut across the upper thigh, and though it wasn't deep, and I had been sure I was well enough to ride, a day or so out, I was shivering with an ague and only just barely able to stay in the saddle.

We were less than a mile from Penliath, someone said, and Einon listened to them. Despite every argument I could muster, he gave orders to turn aside on the road, and we came, at length, to a place I really could have gone a lifetime without ever seeing again.

Penliath Keep was, of course, much smaller than I remembered, and the hall I'd thought such an echoing, treasured space, I saw it now as simply ordinary, and in no way a place of any magnificence.

The steward was pleasant and courteous, not seeming put out by our arrival one whit. There was no healer, but she sent down to the village for an old woman whose herb-lore she trusted, and who turned out to be more than competent enough for my needs.

We only stayed two nights. Two nights too many, for me.

It was not just my dreams, which were harrowing enough. I could explain those away as the symptoms of my wound.

It wasn't that I feared my secret past would come out. Within a very few moments of our arrival, I realized that none of the servants and few of the villagers remembered my curse-laden childhood, and that the years had worn away those edges for them, anyway. My position as a friend of the new duke held promise for them, and they were doing well enough out of it so far that they were happy to forget those old tales.

I could feel the evil, though, seeping from the walls. It was so clear and present to me that I found it unbelievable that the others did not feel it. I thought I might be, underneath it all, a coward, then, that everyone else felt this smearing of wickedness that clung to the very stones of the place, and were simply unafraid to walk its shadows.

But oblique questions and sideways queries brought home to me that no one, not the people who lived here, nor any of my friends and guests, felt even the tiniest bit of it. It was clear my courtly companions thought Penliath a pleasant little place, and that, someday, when things were quieter, they would be happy to break journeys here, envisioning me as their complacent host, serving up wine and fresh-killed venison in my little hall.

On the second night, the herb-woman came late. She'd been making up a sort of infusion for me, for the morrow, to stave off the last of my fevers. I woke out of a doze to see her, kneeling at the fire in the little grate, deeply engrossed in watching the flames.

They'd put me in my mother's old room. I had wanted to protest, but some of the old caution had come back and made me wary. I had gritted my teeth and did not scream out my childish terrors.

"Child of darkness…" Did I imagine her words? "Child of darkness, you are called and called again."

I might have been dreaming, but I didn't think so. The fire crackled, giving off a shower of sparks, but the old one, she didn't even twitch.

"The theft of a daughter, it cuts at the roots of the world."

I woke up in the morning, and there was nothing in the wide world over that could have made me stay there a moment longer. I hid the pain that weight on my injured leg gave me, I willed my nerves and sinews against the last shivers of my fever, and I convinced Einon that we shouldn't, couldn't, mustn't linger any longer, and we rode out before midday, and I never, ever even thought about returning there.

***

We weren't back in the courtyard at Rhwyn a single grain of the glass, and I wasn't even fully out of the saddle, when Arlais was at my elbow, asking where on earth I'd been and where was Eardith?

"Hold up," I said, grabbing onto the reins. "Hold up, Arlais. You're making Balefire jumpy."

She backed off, a little, till one of the stable lads came and led the poor horse off to the stables.

"Well, then," I said. "What's the trouble?"

"Where is Eardith? I haven't seen her since," she paused, looking bewildered, "since last evening. I think. She's not in her room. No one's seen her at all."

"Calm down. She spent last night at the cottage. She had things she wanted to see to, she said."

"You talked to her this morning, then?"

"No, she lent me her room. I was here all night."

"But Balefire - you went back down for him. You must have seen her then?"

102

"Owain sent someone for Balefire," I said. "Early this morning, I expect."

"What servant? Where are they?" She was, if anything, more frantic now.

"I've no idea. Arlais, what's all this about?"

She drew a breath. It was like how you take a gulp of wine, when you need a moment to gather yourself, before you give someone some evil tidings.

"She said we needed to talk. Alone, just the two of us. And that we should meet early, in the garden, before anyone else was about."

"And she didn't show?" That was a little odd, but not something I would have worried over, and I said so. Eardith might have got distracted and lost track of time. She did, sometimes, when she got interested in something.

"N-no…that is, I don't know." Arlais suddenly grew rather pink. "I don't know what happened. I remember talking to her. And then - I don't know. I don't remember. I don't remember even going to my bed. I mean, I was thinking of going, because it was so hot and loud, and - I think I remember being on the stairs, but… I only woke a glass ago. And no one has seen her. Anywhere."

I considered this. But an abundance of wine can do that sort of thing to you, leaving you with only the haziest outline of whole evenings. One's companions are usually only too happy to fill in the gaps for you, of course.

"Well, then. Let's find whoever went down to get my horse, if that will ease your mind."

That proved less simple than it would have seemed. It took a long time to find someone who could remember as far back as early dawn, and Arlais was getting visibly more anxious, but at last we ran the stable-boy to ground, just finishing with the stacking up of all the tack from the morning's hunt.

"Oh, aye, she was there," he said.

"Was she well?" I'd created, in my mind, a plausible story to cover Arlais' agitation. "She complained last night of indigestion."

"Well, I didn't speak to her, like."

"But she looked well?"

He hesitated. From one of the stalls down the way, I could hear Guerin, telling Shadow what a fine, strong, brave boy he was, to come through the colic so well.

"I didn't see her, altogether," said the boy, finally. "The door were shut up tight, you know? But she were in there, right enough. I could hear her voice. Praying, like. And she had a fire going."

I turned to Arlais. "We'll walk down and see her. Will that content you?"

If I'd been her, I'd have heard - and resented - the patronizing note in my voice. But she was too focused on her own concerns.

"We should go now," she said, "We should just go. And not a word to anyone."

At that moment, of course, Guerin walked out of Shadow's stall. He looked at the pair of us, and he smiled that smile, the one that never boded well.

"Here, now," he said. "What's afoot?"

"Just thinking of taking my spears back to the cottage," I said hastily. "Indeed, we ought to be going, so…"

The smile deepened. Arlais was, if anything, more upset than before, and she was hopping impatiently from one foot to the other, in a fury to be moving.

"You might want to collect those spears before you go," he pointed out. "Or, of course, you could tell me what is really going on. Your choice."

Apparently, leaving no word with anyone did not cover Guerin of Orleigh, because Arlais immediately began to pour out a somewhat incoherent summary of her worries to him.

I understood it, I suppose. He was the heir of Orleigh and the duke's man and they'd spent days on the road together. She trusted him. Most people did. It was one of his more lethal qualities.

He listened patiently, and then looked at me.

"It is a bit odd," I said. "She seemed well enough last night, and it wasn't so late when she left."

"Right," he said. "It's a fine day, and we fancy a walk. " He gestured casually towards the yard. "After you."

Chapter Eighteen

The laneway to Eardith's cottage lay opposite the little roadside shrine on the far side past the village.

It had only been the merest chance, that first night, that at the very moment I had been riding by, desperate for shelter from the threatening storm, Eardith had taken her lantern to light her way to the privies by the garden. I'd seen the light, bobbing faintly in the darkness, and then I'd noticed a break in the trees where the path began, and turned toward it, in hopes of at least getting Balefire a little protection from the incoming weather.

Otherwise, I expect I'd have gone on that extra half-mile and stumbled into Rhwyn village. I probably would have pounded on the innkeep's door, and she might even have woken up, and the next morning, or the one after that, I'd have taken the road south and hired on as an unknown trooper in Birais' garrison at Glaice.

But there had been that light in the darkness.

Our walk down from the manor was a quiet one. Arlais was lost in her own thoughts, and Guerin, after a few abortive attempts at lighthearted conversation, had mercifully shut up as well. There had been only a couple of people awake and moving in the village, just Joss' mother wearily dragging an armload of hay down to the sheep-cote, and Briega's eldest shooing a couple of goats out onto the green. I suspected most everyone else was still nursing sore heads from last night's excesses.

The road was utterly empty of folk by the time we reached the outskirts, where it began to curve northward. It was very quiet; you could hear birdsong and the chuckling of the brook, and a soft breeze among the trees, all quite pleasantly spring-like and peaceful.

It was only when I saw the shrine that any misgivings truly disturbed my heart.

It was the usual half-circle of three stone uprights. You see them everywhere: one Mother-stone, flanked by the two smaller ones representing Her in Her other attributes, and then the little flat offering slab, where the villagers could leave flowers or grain or little trinkets, in supplication or in thanks.

There was, this time, the stiffening corpse of a little squirrel, blood still brilliantly red and congealing, against the flat, grey stone.

In some places, they still do offer Her blood. In some places, She is still, first and foremost, Destroyer of Worlds.

But not in Keraine. Never in Keraine, and especially not in Dungarrow, where we had had to fight so hard to be free of that darker, more implacable vision of Her, and rein in that will to power from the priesthood.

Arlais stopped suddenly in her tracks. It was not, apparently, a common sight for her, either.

In that moment before I saw her face, I'd been hoping that this was something that made sense to her, that it wasn't a confirmation of her fears, but that hope was dashed immediately.

She was suddenly pale, her breathing was short and raspy, and she seemed unable to look away from the little carcass on the stone. After a long moment, Guerin took her arm and turned her away, away to where the path began, and without any words at all, we started slowly walking down the lane.

The stable-boy might have seen smoke leaking from the thatch, but any fire Eardith had had going had long since died out. He'd said the door was shut tight, but it was ever so slightly ajar now. For just a little bit, this gave me a kind of vague hope, although every nerve in my body knew already at least partly what we would find.

Guerin looked over Arlais' head at me; he still had hold of her arm, and I didn't need him to say anything. I knew that whatever was inside, he didn't want her to see it, at least not without some warning. She had been living on her fears for hours by now, and any sort of shock would do her no good at all.

I walked alone to the door. Even before I reached it, I could see that things were not well within. An overturned, broken bench was clearly visible just a foot or two inside the threshold. But worse: there was a smell about, a smell I knew all too well. The stench of death. And underneath that, there was something else. Something alien, and chill, and oddly familiar.

I pushed, but something was blocking the door and I was fairly sure, from the feel of it, what that something probably was. I put my weight into it, finally, and felt the heft and heard the dragging sound I had expected, as Eardith's body gave way and the doorway widened.

Her throat had been savagely, mercilessly torn away, and she lay in a pool of her own blood, but that was not the worst of it. There were marks, calculated, carved marks cutting away at her wrists and ankles. I wasn't priesthood material, nothing even close, but even I understood what that sort of marking could mean.

The cottage was a shambles, but still out of all that mess, I grasped that something deliberate, something ritually symbolic and organized, had been taking place.

There were three plain, unglazed clay cups, overturned and shattered, with the wine stains still wet and visible on the floorboards.

There were three dark candles, beeswax ones, not tallow, and two were knocked clean out of their undecorated wooden holders, and I noticed, too, almost mechanically, that our larger cauldron lay on its side amid all this, and that a noisome, black-looking mess of oily debris had spilled out of it, to join itself to that thickening pool of blood.

I turned away, backing out of the door, and said as quietly and as gently as I was able,

"It's what we - it's worse than we feared."

Arlais seemed to almost fold in on herself, with a sad, forlorn sigh. Her body swayed a little and both Guerin and I thought that she was going to faint, but here she once again surprised me.

She drew in a long, shuddering breath, and straightened.

I've seen soldiers do this. When they're truly frightened, when they're outnumbered and they know that this, surely, will be their last battle, but they cannot possibly avoid the inevitable, something in them faces up to that, and lends them a last, unknown strength.

It was just the same for Arlais. She looked up and met my eyes and said, tonelessly, "I see. Well, then."

I said, "You needn't look. It isn't... it isn't pretty. But... there are things in here I don't understand."

She shook her head, as if to clear it.

"I need to see, then, don't I?"

It was all right for me, I thought. It was all right for Guerin. We'd seen the ugly aftermath of battles. We'd witnessed the wild results of long sieges, and the beastliness soldiers can display in those frustrating, angry victories. This was worse, of course, but only because of the circumstances and the lack of any obvious reasons for it, and we'd get over it. I wondered if Arlais ever could.

But I moved away as she walked to the cottage door, and silently let her pass. It was, in the end, not my decision. It was arcane, priestly stuff, and she was, as she had been at pains to establish, not a child anymore.

At Arlais' direction, we touched as little as we could. One of the candles had rolled away off towards the hearth, but when Guerin stretched out his hand, unthinking, to retrieve it, she barked a rather sharp command at him to leave it be, and we were both careful, after that, not to disturb anything without her permission.

She was composed and business-like now, but it was a control made up, I thought, of equal parts expertise in occult lores and a barely submerged terror. Whatever had happened here, Arlais understood enough of it to be not merely horrified, but almost paralyzed with fear, and that in turn made the two of us as jumpy as woodland deer in autumn.

She crouched beside Eardith's body for a long while, peering intently at the marks, before looking just as closely at the rest of the room.

"Is there oak growing hereabouts?" she asked, after a bit.

"I think so, yes."

"Can you cut me a green branch, about like so?" She held out her hands about the length of a hunter's long knife apart.

I went out. There was an oak at the bottom of the field, but I had to shinny up to the first strong branch to get what she wanted.

109

She had found a plain tallow candle in the clutter, and the broom, and she had brought out, from some pocket under her skirts, a bit of chalky stone and was drawing, laboriously, around the mess and the corpse, a careful circle.

She motioned us away. We went to stand over by the hearth, as far back as we could. She stood as close to the centre of her circle as she was able, without touching any part of Eardith or the blood or that disgusting mess from the pot. She lit the candle and set it carefully down, and began to sweep at the ooze and the carnage, whispering all the while in a language I could not even slightly understand.

The sweeping, I could see, was not meant to actually tidy things up. In the dimness I could see a bluish glow forming on the broom. It leapt, in long shards of coldfire, onto the liquids and onto Eardith, and slowly, the all-pervasive stench of death and wickedness that had filled our nostrils began to ease.

Still muttering her strange words, she set the broom aside and lit the oak branch from the candle. Being so spring-young and green, I wouldn't have bet on its catching hold, but it did, it smoldered a sickly yellow in the dim light, and Arlais laid it, gently, tenderly, onto Eardith's cold breast.

It flamed up suddenly, quickly, brightly orange-red, and then, just as suddenly, collapsed into ash.

Her voice rose in a final, still incomprehensible invocation, and then she leant over and blew the ash away, and I could feel it now, the sense that whatever evil had invaded this place was gone, banished, fled.

Not that it mattered. It still wasn't a place I wanted to be. Not now, not ever again.

Arlais agreed.

"You should collect your things, if they weren't touched." she said. "We can't move her ourselves, but it should be safe enough now for some others to move her body. And soon. The cottage, well, I don't know. It should be burned."

I found and righted the ladder that went to the little loft above. It was mine, insofar as anything in this place had belonged to me, shared with the strings of onions and garlic, bunches of dried herbs and a couple of hams gifted from grateful villagers for a healing or a safe birth.

I didn't own much, and because I had never properly decided to stay, I had continued to mostly live out of my saddlebags. All I really needed to do was to collect up a few odd bits like my whetstone and a pair of bone dice, stuffing them blindly in on top of my spare shirts and tunics, to roll up my winter cloak and pick up my shield from the corner, and I was done.

Chapter Nineteen

From almost the first moment we were back at the manor, Lady Ilona took charge, and I, for one, was thankful for it.

She was visibly shocked and she was truly grief-stricken. She was grateful and full of praise for whatever it was that Arlais had done - they used some strange and unfamiliar terms in discussing it - and mixed in with Ilona's praise was a slightly perplexed, querying note. She seemed heretofore not to have been aware that this sort of lore was precisely what Arlais was expert in, but she herself, Ilona said firmly, was the only person who was capable of dealing with the body and its disposal, and she needed to be sure that things were done properly.

It was what Eardith would have wanted, she said, sadly.

Arlais merely nodded and fell silent. She had been so obviously exhausted after the ritual that we hadn't been sure she would make it all the way back to the keep, and now she seemed barely able to stand on her own. With Birais' authority backing him and under Ilona's direction, Owain assembled a small party to do the heavy lifting, and we three were left behind to sort ourselves out.

First, we had to deal with Lady Delwen. She was clearly upset, and not merely at the news of Eardith's death, or even the little that had already leaked out regarding the circumstances. There was now the difficult prospect of trying to find a place for me to sleep. She'd given away Eardith's room that morning to the pair who had bunked in with Guerin, on the strength of her understanding that Eardith would be happier at home now that all these formalities were done.

Her distress was further compounded by the fact that sometime between yesterday and today, Owain or someone had obviously explained to her exactly who I was, and she was trying to think back to see if she had ever been less than courteous to me.

She hadn't been, insofar as I was likely to notice, and I tried to tell her that. I also pointed out that I was quite happy to bed down in the hall with the guards and the servants, but she seemed on the verge of tears at this, until I looked at Arlais, standing a little apart and lost in thought, and said,

"Arlais - that is, the holy one's had a shock, she shouldn't be alone. If she's willing, and there's a spare pallet, I can share her chamber."

Arlais roused at the sound of her name, blinked, and said, "Oh. Yes. That's a good idea," in a tone that suggested she hadn't really heard a word. Guerin smiled mirthlessly at both of us and picked up my shield and my cloak where he'd dropped them. I grabbed my saddlebags, and we herded her towards the stairs.

Once in her room, Arlais did collapse, more or less. We got her as far as the bed, where she curled into a ball and began to tremble uncontrollably.

"Wine," said Guerin, firmly. I nodded.

While he was gone, I set my cloak and my shield into the far corner, and leaned my sword against it. Arlais was still shaking, and her breath was coming in little, hiccuppy jerks, but all I could think of to do was to cover her with a wool blanket and hope that Guerin got back soon.

When he reappeared, it was with two servants, one manhandling a straw pallet and another carrying two coverlets. It took a few minutes to get it sorted out. The servant in charge of the bedding seemed bent on being more than ordinarily inefficient about it, and the one who had carried the coverlets stood in the middle of the room, staring in fascination at the sight of a holy servant of the Mother reduced to quivering jelly.

We got rid of them, finally, and Guerin poured out the wine, handing one cup to me and taking the other to the bed, where, in the same low, soothing voice he'd used with Shadow, he coaxed Arlais first into a sitting position, and then, to drink some of the wine.

I opened my saddlebags, hunting for a clean shirt and my spare tunic.

I'm not a neat person, as a rule. In the beginning, I had owned nothing, of course, at least nothing that needed taking care of, and at Gorsedd, my clothes were collected and cleaned by others. If I dropped them carelessly on the floor, they got folded and laid back in my clothes-chest for me, and the very worst was that the servant might complain to Lady Ilona, and I would be asked to try not to be so inconsiderate. At Dungarrow, the servants did not complain, or if they did, it wasn't to anyone willing to press the point directly.

At Eardith's cottage, of course, I'd been a kind of guest, and mindful of being there on sufferance and determined not to be a burden, I had done my own washing as best I could and as rarely as I could get away with. I had been careful about not leaving any visible mess that could inconvenience my benefactor, but I was still careless, and somewhat clueless about the niceties: I never bothered to do more than stuff my things willy-nilly back into the saddlebags.

When I opened them up now, though, my shirts and tunics were carefully and meticulously folded in the bags, and separated, too, with the two shirts and my padded arming tunic in one and my spare tunic in the other, on top of my mail shirt. And when I put my hand on the topmost linen shirt, I felt something hard and a little heavy, and not shirt-like at all.

There was that faintly queasy feeling at the pit of my stomach again. I let the shirt slide out halfway from the saddlebag, and the cloth fell partly open at the folds.

It was small, and square, that thing wrapped inside. It had a leather cover, blackened with age. I'd seen it occasionally before, a little book that Eardith sometimes read or wrote in. I had assumed it was an herbal or some such, a record of her healing cures or notes to calculate which village rituals needed to be done and when.

But even before I laid a finger on it now, I knew that it couldn't be something so innocuous or innocent. It was important, and in view of the scene in the cottage, possibly dangerous, too.

There was, just then, a commotion outside. We could hear it from the open window which looked down onto the courtyard, the muffled sounds of the jingle of horses' bridles and the shouting for the stablehands to come for the horses, drifting up as if it were just an ordinary day.

"The Lady's back," said Arlais, softly. "It's done, then."

I slid the shirt back into the bag, stuffing it down past the other one, and pushed the whole mess into the corner near my shield. I couldn't seem to order my thoughts, they were streaming past me like a river in flood, and all I could think was that I needed time and quiet to make some kind of sense of this.

Time and quiet that I didn't seem destined to have. Moments later, there was someone scratching at the door, to tell us the king hoped the Lady Arlais was recovered, and that please would we join them all in the hall.

A king's politely-worded request is not easily dismissed, but Arlais, although she looked somewhat better than she had a half-glass before, was still pale and weary.

"I can easily stay," I said. "You go, Guerin. I can manage."

Guerin disagreed. It seemed unlike him to prefer nurse-maiding Arlais to eating a decent dinner, and we began to argue, under the cover of what was best for Arlais, as if this was the single most important decision we might ever be making.

"Stop it!"

We'd forgotten all about her, actually.

She swung herself off the bed. "We'll all go down."

I looked her over. There was some colour in her cheeks, now, and she seemed considerably improved. Was it my imagination, then, that saw in her recovery something more? A thread of excitement, of anticipation, a renewed resolve?

"If you're sure, Arlais?" Guerin sounded genuinely concerned. I wondered if maybe my suspicions were in all the wrong direction. Maybe he was sleeping with her? And then I wondered why it was I should care.

"I'm fine. At least, I will be, if you don't give me the pip with your quarrels."

Halfway down the hallway, I stopped.

"Damn. I need my eating knife, it's still on my sword-belt. Don't wait up. I'll only be a grain or two."

It wasn't the most convincing of excuses. I could tell that Guerin had half a mind to follow me back, but Arlais was nodding and already heading down the corridor to the stairs, and after a moment, he shrugged and followed her.

I slipped back into the room. Whatever had happened, only Eardith could have put that book in with my things. I couldn't imagine why she would, and until I knew that, it seemed obvious that its existence needed to remain hidden. Wrapped in my spare shirt in my saddlebags was not a good description of "hidden".

***

The mood in the hall was somber when I arrived, to say the least.

It wasn't just the death. If she'd died of some sickness or accident, Eardith would have been missed and mourned, certainly. For all her brusque ways and lack of gentle speech, people here had been used to her, had counted on her and loved her, even, I suppose, in their own way.

Burning the cottage down, well, that alone would have set off the rumors, of course. Country people, poor people, they don't waste a perfectly good building without dire need.

The additional rituals Ilona had insisted on, although she'd managed them alone and left the others outside, they hadn't gone unremarked, either. The preparation for those had been uncommon enough that all the solemn oaths and dire threats in the world could not have kept the little crew that accompanied her down there silent. Not wholly so and not for long. By morning, I reckoned, the whole of the valley would know.

And now, the whispers, the furtive looks, the warding signs, all this reminded me uncomfortably of my long-ago childhood. It wasn't enough that this time, none of it was aimed at me. It wasn't really aimed at anyone, or anywhere, just out at the nebulous, the unknowable, the frightening realm of otherness that had invaded Rhwyn Vale. But they were still a chilling reminder of what catastrophes my presence seemed to bring, everywhere I went.

Ilona still looked the picture of grief, but she stopped briefly to speak to Arlais. Even from a distance, it was obviously a friendly chat, the older, wiser holy one taking the time to reassure a less-experienced colleague. Arlais seemed quite recovered now, even smiling a little and blushing, because it looked as if Ilona was all praise for her regarding the things she had done in the cottage.

116

And then the Lady came and sat by me.

It was, to me, no more than her usual kindness. She said that she was sure, having shared Eardith's cottage so long, I must be sorrowing deeply, and it seemed prudent to agree with this. In fact, I was sorry that Eardith was gone, quite apart from the horror of it. I would miss her, and that surprised me into sincerity.

She smiled sadly and patted my hand. Time, she said, and she was sure I had learned this for myself, these last years, time, it healed all things.

Then she began reminiscing, about how the two of them had been girls together on the holy isle, had Eardith ever told me about those days? And your mother, too, she said. She was younger than they, but she'd been there.

It was at that point that I became acutely aware that underneath the very real grief, underneath the mourning and the reminiscence, the Lady was watching me, watching and studying me so closely and in a manner that was so alert and narrow that the hairs on the back of my neck literally rose, like a cat's.

And so I was ready for it, in a way, when she at last turned her talk to the way the cottage had been, when we first entered. What had I seen? Had any of us, had Arlais especially, touched anything, disturbed anything, taken anything away?

I gave her simple answers, and she did not seem to find that strange.

My descriptions of the state of the room were a warrior's descriptions, accurate, factual and without any underlying conjecture, because I had long been a warrior, and that is how the training goes.

The ritual had looked to me like many another, save for the coldfire and the way the oak branch had burst into flame, and when she asked about it, I said as much.

I had always striven hard to present myself as an ordinary person exactly like a thousand others, and my observations were bound to be simple ones. That was what she expected, after all.

She asked casually, almost as an afterthought, whether I'd left anything of my own behind, saying kindly that she would make good any losses. And when I said only that I wasn't missing either of my shirts or my

117

second-best tunic and thanked her for her kindness, she seemed satisfied, and moved away to retrieve her wine cup, to sit beside the king and Owain, and to discuss more important matters than the unlikely grief of a practiced killer.

I thought long and hard about the things she had said and the questions she had asked. Slipping them in between commiserations and queries about my own emotional state, there had still been a kind of pattern to them, and a probing intensity buried deep beneath that tone of affectionate concern.

I rose and went to the fire. The evening was a fine one, and doors of the hall stood open to the warmth of spring, and I was cold, so cold, I didn't think I would ever be warm again.

Chapter Twenty

The hall still seemed unnaturally quiet, considering the number of people inhabiting it, and the roast venison notwithstanding, it was not a merry meal. People kept their voices hushed, partly out of respect for a death, but also, I thought, because they were being careful not to touch on anything uncanny, at least not where their betters could hear them, and this rather put a damper on discussion.

Derryth, who had a fine voice, sang, at Owain's request, a haunting little refrain about returning spring. It had been one of Eardith's favourites. Her other favourite had been a rollicking, bawdy old song about a farmer who had an amorous yearling sheep, but I could quite see why Owain hadn't requested that one.

Afterwards, Arlais and I had watched Guerin win a fair sum at dice from one of the king's captains, and then wandering, by some strange, mutual consent, drifting together aimlessly towards the stairs without speaking a word.

I stopped a moment on the threshold of her chamber and saw that everything was in its own place, exactly as we'd left it.

Almost.

The tilt of my saddlebags against the wall was less acute, the folded blanket hung over the edge of the bed by an inch or so more than it had before, and the straw pallet the servants had brought was further away from the wall than when we'd left to walk down to the hall.

I moved over to the window, glancing out as if I was checking the weather. There was nothing to see there, not if you didn't know precisely where and what to look for. Rhwyn was old, and at irregular intervals all along the inner sill and the outer stone coping of most of the windows, there were slim spaces, cracks where time and weight and weather had moved the masonry ever so slightly apart. Delwen often complained of the drafts that the aging walls allowed in on winter nights.

A few minutes later, Guerin arrived, noisy and boisterous.

"I remembered you ladies would still have some wine," he said, grinning. He came through the door and shut it loudly behind him.

"I need to use the latrines," I said. Even to my own ears, this sounded overloud and a bit false, although it was true, I did need the privies. I'd made sure of it by gulping down a mug of ale I'd had not a thirst for, before the meal had ended.

I could still hear him, when I was out the door and halfway to the stairs, asking in a drunken voice if Arlais had ever been to Kerris, because he didn't believe one word in five what that captain had said about its magnificence.

I was trying to be both casual and careful. It wasn't that easy.

The hall was all but empty now, save for a few servants still clearing away, and the humped shapes of those people not lucky enough to have a proper bed for the night. I walked the length of the open space hearing no more than a snore or two.

In the yard, it was even quieter: you could hear the crickets and the occasional owl. I stepped into the latrines and made the usual noises one makes in a latrine. I did the usual things one does in a latrine.

Still, there was just silence.

I walked back out towards the hall and only then, because I was watching for it and straining my ears for the slightest sound, I caught the merest shadow of a figure moving beyond me back towards the latrines, heard the faintest of footfalls, and sighed inwardly. I had not been imagining things.

No one followed me back to the hall. There was no one behind me on the stairs, and I fumbled unnecessarily at the chamber door trying to make certain there was no one lurking about in the corridor. Guerin and Arlais were quieter, now, but they were still making cheerful conversation as if it were the most ordinary of evenings.

I shut the door behind me. They both looked up, and Guerin, still acting the slightly inebriated flirt, said, "Ah, you're back. Care for a game?" and rattled the dice in his hand and threw them.

They came up snake's eyes. Never a good thing.

"Sure." I said.

He picked up the dice again. An ordinary evening, I thought. Just two old friends, gambling and drinking the night away.

Except, of course, we weren't old friends, not really, not ever truly friends, and even discounting what the Lady might be thinking of us, closeted up here together as if the age-old feud didn't even come into it, I was sure this was one of the least safe things I could be doing right now.

"Stakes?" he said, smiling. That old, familiar smile.

"I don't have a bean. But I'll bet you a cup of wine you can't throw snake's eyes again."

Guerin threw. It wasn't snake's eyes.

"Double your bet for twos?" He handed me the dice.

I tossed them out. They were twos.

"The demon's own luck, damn you."

We poured out more wine.

"I can spot you a beggar's bit or three," he offered. "Make it more interesting."

"All right. Bet you can't roll a dragonback in any combination."

But he did: a four and a two, and he laughed.

"Beat that, then. All or nothing?"

"Don't be daft," I muttered. "No one's got that much luck."

I threw.

Double dragons.

"You see?" He was looking at me with an intensity I had seen in him so seldom before, and once it had been when we'd stood together on a stairway, ready to risk everything on my ability to kill a seasoned warrior who stood in Einon's way.

"You should trust your luck more often."

Did I only imagine it? That the room had come alive with unspoken words, with that odd, prickly feel of the air before a springtime storm?

It came to me then, that I did trust Guerin, in a way. He was Einon's, as surely as I was, and maybe more. Whatever he did would have

Dungarrow's interests at its core, and Orleigh is famous for nothing if not their steadfast, almost maniacal devotion to their sworn word.

But then there was Arlais. I looked over at her, curled up back on the bed, watching us. She seemed no more than mildly interested. What side was she on? She had been annoyed by Ilona, but then, she'd been just as angry at Eardith, earlier on. And this evening, she'd seemed to have made her peace again with the Lady of Gorsedd.

She knew things. Too many things. Things, it occurred to me, that she was really too young to have been trusted with. Things that normally take a lifetime to learn, things that even Eardith had seemed to have been unaware of.

I wished that I could have had Eardith back, if only for a half of a glass, to ask her what was going on. Or even who I could trust, since I didn't, apparently, trust myself. There was a game here that I knew nothing of. The only thing I was sure of was that Eardith had died for it, and I needed to know why.

Finally, I just shrugged, drained off my wine at a gulp and said, "I'm for bed. They'll all be waking early, if the king wants to be on the road home at a decent hour."

"He's not going anytime soon," Guerin informed me. "All this, and we had to tell him about the wolves, too, it's got him spooked. He means to get to the bottom of it."

"Damn his eyes," I said. "What's it got to do with him?"

"He thinks it's some Camrhyssi plot. You know how they are. Always messing about with dark rites, and trying to imitate the ancients. Birais thinks it is some of their priests, looking for a way to take the House of Machyll down and overrun the kingdom."

"That seems a bit farfetched," I said. "Rhwyn's an unlikely place for an invasion."

"Is it?" This was from Arlais. "The Lady agrees with you, of course. "

I wasn't imagining the tension, now. It was as real and as palpable as the wine-jar beside me. The three of us, squaring off like barnyard cats. I found myself torn between hysterical giggles and a burning desire to tell them both everything, to hand that damned book over to Arlais and wash my hands of it all.

One of the candles caught a slight breeze from the open window. It flickered and went out and that prickling tension between us spluttered out with it.

Guerin shrugged. He picked up the dice and said, "Well, and you're right, of course. It's late enough, and we'll all do better for some sleep."

In the darkness, I could feel the questions, swirling around me. I had no idea what to do, and it seemed to me that my safest bet was to do nothing at all.

Feargal came into Dungarrow Castle two days later, to submit to judgment, to plead clemency of his duke, and I called the challenge. He had looked so dire, so shadowed and tormented, and so unlike his laughing self, but what did I care for that? He had accepted everything, and I did not see, could not let myself see, the sorrow and the bewilderment and the despair in every inch of him. He had stood out on the field, knowing I would kill him. It was in his eyes, and in mine. There could be nothing else. We both knew it.

And not even Einon's simple request, that voice asking me to back down, just this once, to trust him, just a little, to wait for proper justice, to not do this thing - it could not stop me.

I barely heard him, there was so much murder in my heart. Some part of me knew this was another ending, that whatever life I had had before would be utterly and completely destroyed, but it didn't matter. It couldn't matter, not against the pain inside.

And I walked out and looked at the man I'd wedded and bedded, a man I'd laughed with and gambled with and drank with, a man I'd fought beside and trusted, had known for the best part of my life and called my friend, and I felt nothing, nothing at all but the emptiness of my loss, and I killed him in as painfully efficient a manner as I could.

Not even his last words could have moved me, then.

But they moved me now.

Chapter Twenty-Two

Arlais was already up and about when I woke, and she looked, if not cheerful, at least no longer in that state of complete nervous exhaustion, and she seemed determined to behave as if yesterday had never been.

I trailed behind her down to the hall, still trying to shake my head free of the dreams and memories. I filled a mug of ale and collected a couple of oatcakes and wandered out into the courtyard, still shut up inside my own head and preoccupied with my own confusion. I couldn't even form intelligent questions, as far as I could tell, let alone begin looking for answers.

I nearly fell over Lannach, who was sitting in front of the doorway in very nearly the same place as I had been heading for.

He rose.

I tensed. I didn't need another fight, not now, not when my mind was all on more crucial things.

"Lady Caoimhe." he said. His voice was strained and stiff and it was as much a question as a greeting.

"Lady Caoimhe," he repeated.

"Yes?"

"His Grace asked me, well, told me, really, that I must make amends."

He was pale and shamefaced with it, and he'd lost that self-satisfied look of the practice ground bully entirely. It came to me now, how very young he was, and how he'd likely never been thwarted before, not in any real desires, until last night.

"There's nothing," I said, calmly, "that you need amend, for me. You lost a match, nothing more. There's no shame in trying, nor in losing, either."

"You could have killed me, though."

"Well, yes. But to what purpose? Although," I paused, thinking that teaching him to perhaps consider an action a little more before he committed to it might be no bad thing, "you could try coming up with

Chapter Twenty-Three

Rhwyn boasted very few of what Lord Uln had once disparagingly referred to as "northern comforts", but they did have a bath house of sorts. It hadn't been constructed with the idea that over fifty soldiers might need it at once, of course, and after two hours of beating up everyone I could talk or trick into match-ups, I could see I'd have to wait my turn a good long while. It was simply bad luck for me that by the time I got back from dumping my mail shirt and arming tunic off and collecting some cleaner things to wear, I wound up stuck next to Guerin in the lines.

I hadn't seen Arlais since I'd left her in the hall that morning. She hadn't been in our room when I'd gone to change before heading to the practice ground, nor was she there when I'd gone back after. I had been pushing both her and Lady Ilona's very existences out of my mind, to be honest, because the truth was they had become the lynch-pins of the problems I was trying to avoid.

He started in on it immediately, though. When had I last seen Arlais? How had she been?

"Guerin," I said, "I don't know. I just told you. She seemed fine, and I haven't seen her since we went into the hall for breakfast, and no, she wasn't ailing."

And what's it to you, anyway? I wondered, again, if they were lovers.

His attitude, though, wasn't very lover-like. He was worried, but not in a way that suggested the personal. It was almost as if, like me, he suspected her of some ulterior motive, and needed to keep track of her movements. Or, perhaps, that she had some knowledge that he wanted, and he was hoping to prise it out of her somehow.

He didn't answer. He was looking down the line and suddenly, he straightened and said, in a low voice, "Look sharp, Caoimhe."

I followed his gaze. Birais was just leaving the bath house, his hair still dripping wet. It was like him, I thought, absently, to wait his turn here along with his troops, when he could have easily pre-empted the first spot, or demanded a tub of hot water in his chamber. He was known for gestures like this, though, acting like one soldier among many, instead of standing on his privileges as king.

Well, and Einon did much the same thing, when he was in the field. It's a good investment. The rank and file love it, and that makes them more willing to risk death for you.

The king hadn't come near me on the practice ground, but I had noticed that he was watching me. I suspected that at least two of my fights had been because he had told those soldiers to offer me bouts. I wasn't even particularly surprised. After Lannach's claims about my overblown reputation, it seemed probable that Birais was mentally tallying what I was actually capable of with what he, too, might have heard.

But out past the king, across from the bath house, over where that unused cow-byre stood, where Delwen had had to house some of the extra soldiers crowding her home, there were two other people, deep in conversation. And really, they wouldn't have been the two people I would have thought even knew each other, much less had anything at all in common.

Arlais was moving away from the man, and disappearing around the corner of the cow-byre wall now. Cowell watched her go, then turned back towards the bath house line-up. He could see me clearly, he could see me watching him, but he seemed uncaring, leaning stolidly against the wattle and daub walls with his arms folded, going nowhere.

"That," said Guerin, "isn't a good sign."

It shocked me, a little, that his train of thought ran so close to my own. But he seemed to be making a fairly big assumption about where I stood in this, I thought. For all he knew, I could be as much a part of this mystery as Arlais and Cowell seemed to be. Or was this just more misdirection? One enormous feint before the sword fell from a new angle?

I didn't want to believe it, though I couldn't have, had anyone asked, given a clear reason why. I simply didn't want to believe that Guerin was a part of some underhanded deal with magic and mysteries because it was idiotic and ludicrous, or so I told myself.

He might be mischievous in his habit of putting you on the spot in a political discussion, he might trip you up on your own internal contradictions with an innocent-sounding question, he might even force an avoidable quarrel by those needle-sharp comments thrown lazily out just to amuse himself, but Orleigh dealt in open certainties, in steel-bright honour and in the here-and-now, not in shadowy realms and smiling treacheries.

I suppose, mainly, that it occurred to me that my fears were taking over, and that this way led only to madness.

"Well," I said, after a bit, "at least you know Arlais is all right."

The bath house was overcrowded, and out of courtesy, people were trying to be quick about things. I lost track of Guerin in the steam and the bodies, and wound up beside the hot water sluice with one of the soldiers who'd kept my wine cup full the other night. He introduced me to a couple of his friends, got someone to make some room in the main tub for me, and loaned me a leather thong to re-tie my braid when the one I'd been using decided to break.

That book, I thought. It's something in that book.

It seemed to me, based on what little I'd picked up from living at Gorsedd and from snippets of talk with Nesta, and with Meryn, too, that it was likely I would not be able to read anything in it. There were secret scripts, apparently, protected writings in ancient tongues, and special sigils that might alter those meanings still further beyond that. Nesta had been struggling to memorize the simpler ones when I'd first gotten to Gorsedd, and I'd been relieved that the Lady hadn't ever seemed to consider that sort of learning for me.

I wouldn't know till I looked at it, though.

Cowell was still watching the bath house. I sketched a little salute as I went by, and he ignored it. It seemed possible his watchfulness was for someone else. Guerin? I turned over the possibility, but there seemed no conceivable reason anyone should want to spy on him, and in any case, it wasn't as if he hadn't seen that little exchange with Arlais or that Cowell was skulking around or hiding in dark corners. Guerin, I decided, could take care of himself.

Our room was empty. I left the door open just enough that I might be able to hear someone in the corridor, got out one of my long knives and went to the window.

Inside the crack, I could just still see the top of the thing. It was only seconds before I'd levered it up just enough to grab the corner of it with two fingers and wheedle it further up and out. Somewhere out by the stairs, I heard voices, and I stuffed the thing into my shirt, grabbed my spare tunic and pulled it on.

I needed to be somewhere quiet and not where anyone would expect to see me. Somewhere no one could come up on me unawares. And luckily, because my on-sufferance status in Rhwyn Vale had occasionally offered me chances at slightly dangerous odd jobs that no one else wanted to do, I knew just the place.

Rhwyn might be small, but it wasn't radically different from any other place I'd lived, really. Still, the manor had been reworked and added to over the years, and at one point, one of the original stone outbuildings of the manor house had disintegrated enough that part of it had been pulled down and rebuilt to connect with the main keep.

It had probably been done in a hurry, and not very well, and last year, when the adjoining hallway had developed some serious leaks, I had been the obvious choice to go up with Gair and help him do a patchwork mending job. Not that I was at all versed in carpentry, stonework or roof tiling, of course, but Owain had felt that it was sufficiently risky a job that Gair might need someone to hand him tools and make sure he didn't slip and fall to his death. Owain was good like that. Most lords wouldn't have given the danger to a local tenant farmer a second thought.

Mostly, I'd tried to not be an additional distraction, and just sat around watching Gair work. But we'd had to access the roof through the makeshift loft space above the rafters, and I'd noticed, the very first day, that the builders hadn't closed everything off up there.

At the end where the loft abutted the main wall, there was the remnant of an old window, a small black well of darkness that led, when I'd later investigated out of simple curiosity and boredom, to the higher ceiling beams of a little store-room that Lady Delwen used as a linens cupboard. No one else seemed to have noticed the gap, which didn't surprise me. People don't often look past their own noses, and rarer still do they look up.

The whole place was quiet enough, just now. Everyone who could be spared for it was busy in the kitchens, trying to come up with yet another meal that was plentiful enough for the number of people now in residence and still suitable for a king. Anyone else was either in the yard or on their own errands. It was about the safest time I might ever have.

I closed the door of the cupboard softly behind me, and used one of the middle shelves as a foothold, swinging noiselessly up onto a roof beam and from there crawling through the dusty, cobwebby opening and on into the loft.

I lit the stubby candle-end I'd brought, pulled out the book, and began to flip through the pages.

It was as I'd expected. For the most part, the spidery script shaped no letters I recognized, and there were odd diagrams and designs that meant nothing, less than nothing to me.

Until I got to the last few pages. Much of what was there was still in that strange writing, but interspersed with that were words I could read.

I wished, afterwards, that I hadn't done this. I wished that Eardith had chosen some other place to hide her secrets. I wished that Ilona had not insisted I learn to read at all. But you can't forget the things you know, just for wishing , can you?

Chapter Twenty-Four

Why did we come? I came for Ilona's sake, or so I say now…but what Ilona wanted, I still am not sure of…power, aye, and maybe just the thrill of it, the risk, the danger…That was Mall as well, too young to think of danger as aught but a spice, and too vain to think of the damage she could do. Or mayhap she did think, and liked it - she was always fey and dark, despite the pretty looks and the silvery laughter…

The men, well, they came because Ilona willed it. Eoghan could not allow Ilona to have more power than he, that would have changed it all. And because he was strong in the craft: we needed him, we thought. And Kevern came because he was besotted with Mall. What she felt - well, who knows? They were bound close by dark things afterwards, and much woe for them in store. If he had not been there, would things have turned out differently? But in the end, it was Ilona who moved us. Left to our own devices, would we have gone so far along that road? I no longer remember.

It matters not. We came and we did the things we did. Things that cannot be undone.

I wish I had never found those scraps of parchment. I wish, having found them, I had burned them, or taken them back to Braide and given them to Reverend Mother. But I was like Ilona then, stubborn and arrogant, the pair of us, thinking only of ourselves and what we could do if we could harness the power in that place, perform the rituals of Gathering and take hold of wider knowledge than the fat, middle-aged teachers we served would allow us access to. And then bringing Mall into it - what were we thinking? Of ourselves, still: the ritual works best with threes…

We took precautions. We were prudent. We did not go near the Well, we stayed in the ruins of the little temple below, thinking the bonds that held the evil would not let that power loose so far. We were fools.

It isn't that he took hold of our pathetic little crafting and twisted it. It isn't that he saw the easy darkness in Mall and took her - as I said, the ritual works best with threes…Eoghan and I, for all he was married to Ilona and her already three months gone with child, and Kevern with her - rage manifest as passion as he watched another mounting Mall and she for all to see not shy about it, so beautifully loathsome as that creature was…And then the quarrel with Eoghan and the flash of the sword, the blood, the blood, and then the long years of secrecy and silence in exchange for the power we'd gained - this was the very least of our wickedness.

We loosed the bonds. Oh, with the power that filled me I closed the circle once more, quenched the fire with words of power, willed every ounce of Goddess-good within me into every additional binding spell I could think of, and he was contained.

But he had seen that he might almost be free. Free enough to work his will on others: we showed him that much, and more besides: He saw the crack in his prison walls and it gave him hope...

And so I stayed. First I said it was to be sure the bindings would hold, and made it seem as if a few days or weeks would suffice, but I knew better. Ilona was too intent on using what she'd gained, she didn't think past that, happy enough, in the end, to be a grieving widow holding lands in charge for her unborn babe and ruling as Lady of Gorsedd and priestess together. She didn't think then, as I did, that I would need to stay always, to watch over Rhwyn Vale, and be sure that he never slipped those bonds again.

Now I fear even more. I grow older, and I feel the power draining away. What will happen when I die? Will the spells I wrought die too? Will he lure others into his evil? He has managed, I think, to snare some others over the years, even before we came, but those were little evils, petty, malicious things. And the year Reverend Mother summoned me back to Braide, something happened then, I'm sure of it. I could feel something was wrong, but then, it was a good harvest, and no ill winds...

***

It's her, I'm sure of it, as sure as I can be. Tall, pale, straight as a reed, with her mother's green eyes, always careful, always watchful, and yet so hard and hollow, as if she had never in her life given way to sadness or passion before, and knew not what it was that ailed her.

And yet more strangely, I feel no evil in her, not but what she speaks aright when she says that there is blood on her hands.

Yet she is that thing's spawn - how can there be no sign of it? How can it not scream to me like the demon's own mother in the darkness?

***

Too much death.

Was it caution or cowardice that stopped my lips?

Or my arrogance, perhaps, even now? It blinded me, convinced me the hand of the Goddess moved these things, persuaded me that I could keep her here and run no risks. That I might learn more and so prevent a greater tragedy.

Like calls to like, or so the ancients said. Is he calling her? Why, then, does she not hear him?

With every death, I feel him grow stronger. It has to stop.

***

Well, and I am a bigger fool than I ever thought.

He saw her. Why did I risk it? He has seen her, and doubtless he knows now what she is.

She seems unchanged, which is odd. But he did not truly reveal himself to her...

The lore says nothing on this. Nothing to the point, at least, only that it is blood he needs, and the right blood at the right time, but no more than that.

Did he get wind of her, somehow, and draw her to him without her awareness? Used her somehow, to gain some power and stray so far afield?

Or does he only suspect? Perhaps he does not yet know for certain.

But how could he not?

***

I can feel the darkness, closing in. He is working his will somehow here, and yet I cannot see how this can be. Not through her, I am certain of that now, or he would have moved against me long since. Night upon night, darkness upon darkness, and no sign at all.

And that babe of a priestess they sent me, what good can she be? Knowledgeable enough, I grant you, but as frail and fragile as an unbaked clay jar. The first tumble and she'll break, I warrant. Or go running back to Braide to let us amend things here if we can.

***

How can he be gaining so much strength now?

Have I kept the bonds, performed the rites, sought out all the learning I could, only to fail at the end?

There must be a way to keep us safe. There are Workings, I know, dark things, so Ilona says, that might contain him. Rites could be performed. Words could be said, that could give us the strength to overcome him.

She knows less than she thinks, though. I know of even darker paths…

But I keep thinking there must be another way. A way not so perilous, not so fraught with risk for all of us, if we should fail.

***

Now I know how stupid I've been. I did not see it, would not see it, I let myself be blinded by friendship and guilt, and shared secrets. How long has she been hugging these evils to herself? How long since she gave herself up to the darkness?

I see the truth now, too late: she will not rest, no, not until every ounce of power belongs to her, she would risk anything, sacrifice anything, pay any cost for this.

As must I, to stop her.

Mother forgive me.

***

This is the lore and the history we were taught, listening since babyhood to singers and storytellers in every hall, at every hearth, all across the land.

Long ago, we had been the Kingdom of Averraine, a great and powerful empire, and our ancestors had been mighty in Craft. But they had been less mighty in wisdom, it seemed, and so the Mother had destroyed their world, and started anew, building us up in righteousness on the ruins the ancients had left behind. There was still potential, but it flowed not in those great rivers of Power to places where any adept might partake of it, but through one's devotion to Her, in rituals and prayers and invocations, and only to those She chose to Gift with it. It was never so strong again, nor as easy to hold or shape, because she loved us too well to ever allow us such dangerous powers again.

And she had cursed the ones who had led to our undoing.

Late at night, the tales were told: shivery, chilling descriptions of how their strongest practitioners had been chained to places that had once been the sites of their greatest achievements. How they lived in shadowy half-worlds, gnawing on the bones of their faded glory, hating

Her, hating us, and longing to be free to wreak some horrible vengeance and drown the world in blood and evil.

Or so the holy ones and the bards say. I think it had been a long time since I'd put any stock into the myth of old Averraine's greatness, at least. People like to imagine a past filled with heroes, ever ready and eager to set things aright.

I thought it might be an uncomfortable way to live.

But the darker things...

Incarnates. Dark shadows of nightmares and madness, sucking out the life from anyone unwary enough to be caught in their web? Creatures that neither lived nor died? Those things?

I believed in them. I knew they were real. I had always known. And now I knew why.

Chapter Twenty-Five

It was dark up there in the loft; my little candle had guttered out long since. I kept having to remind myself to breathe, and I was trying, periodically, not to be noisily sick.

Once, I thought, there had been a time when I had dreamed I was not Kevern's child. Once, I had been young enough to imagine that my true father would suddenly appear to claim me, to carry me off in glory, far away from all that misery. Children love those ancient, hopeful tales.

I hadn't been a child for a long, long time, but in this moment I would have given everything I had ever had and more, to have claimed Kevern as my father still.

The Mother loves her little jokes.

Every creak of a roof beam, every rustle of wind in the eaves, every far-off jangle of muffled sound seemed as loud as a shout in my ear.

And all I could think of was how the Penliath folk had feared and hated me, and made the warding signs, how unfair it had always seemed, and how right they had been to fear me, after all.

Gradually, I recognized that it was growing late in the day, and that my absence was sure to be noticed by someone eventually. I couldn't think anymore.

I had considered a thousand plans and schemes, a thousand fantasies and theories, and one by one I had discarded them all. I had tried to find something solid to cling to, some reason to believe I was not the very essence of an abomination, and I had failed.

It no longer seemed to matter. Nothing did. I had arrived at a state of numbness and complete uncaring.

Be a rock. Be a stone wall. Be no living thing.

And after a while, I shoved the little book into a corner, into the dimness of the eaves. There was still, at the far end, a kind of makeshift set of footholds Gair and I had used, and I used them again, and walked out the little side door into the long end of the courtyard and back up into the hall, just in time for the evening meal.

I passed Cowell, who was standing close to one side of the doors. He frowned at me, puzzled, and then looked away. I ought to have felt something then, at least, and it seemed odd that I did not, but all I did was mark that, yes, it was me he was spying on, and set that knowledge away beside all the other horrible, unfathomable, furtive things I now needed to be aware of.

I skipped the more honoured place I'd been allotted near the king's table and found a couple of my soldier friends from the bath house. I ate the plainer fare that was served down there. Even had I ever been the sort to care, it wouldn't have mattered. Nothing tasted like more than sawdust, and the ale might as well have been brackish water for all I knew of it. My companions joked and laughed and I heard my own voice and my own laughter and I could not, ever afterward, remember a single word of any of it.

My companions had plans. They invited me along. I could see, in my present state, no reason to refuse, and so I floated along on a little tide of soldiers, out the door, right past where Cowell still stood watching, still not even trying to hide it, across the yard and out to the gates, down the lane to Rhwyn village, where the innkeep was preparing to enjoy a windfall business that she would likely not see again in a seven-year.

It was crowded with people sporting the red and gold of the House of Machyll, and Rhwyn's best ale was flowing freely. I recognized the captain who had lost so many copper coins to Guerin the night before, but few of the others made more than the mildest of impressions on me.

The raucous greetings and soldiers' catchphrases rang out around me, well-worn insults and jests so old that even my grandfather would have groaned in boredom to hear them repeated. I sat on a bench with my back to the wall, mechanically swallowing tasteless mouthfuls of ale on cue every few minutes, and let the heat and the noise wash over me, letting it all dull my senses.

It got easier. Somewhere along the way, the last scraps of my horror and revulsion had receded, leaving only the drumming refrain of a single question echoing through me.

Why was I still here?

All my life, I now saw, I had been manipulated, pushed and driven by others' needs and desires. Everything I was, everything I'd done up till now, there was none of it that I could confidently claim as my own, or be sure that any of it had ever been under my control. My very conception had served someone else's ends and I was, when I got right down to it, more furious than frightened.

I should have run, three years ago. I should have run, that very first morning, and kept running, as far from Rhwyn as it was humanly possible to go. I should still run, because whatever evil was in me, it surely could do less harm the further I was from its maker. Something or someone wanted me here, and every grain of the glass longer that I stayed was probably a mistake.

The room seemed smokier than usual, stinging my eyes. I blinked away a moment's blurriness, and took a sip from my mug. Running, I thought, but where?

Right now, I thought, there's ale, and the safety of a crowd. How much harm could I do in all this? I saw that Lannach was here, too. I considered waving to him, but he wasn't looking my way, and I was so tired. I saw that my mug was full again and managed another swallow.

I tried to think where I might run to, but I couldn't recall, just then, why the where might be important, and thought, instead, tomorrow. Tomorrow would be time enough to think it all out. The girl beside me had brought out the dice and I was watching the bone cubes flipping through the air and clattering onto the table, over and over, and the bets were piling up...

I could vaguely remember, later, heading out back to the latrines on unsteady legs. I remember only hazily seeing Cowell walking towards me, and I remember beginning to ask him why in all the nine hells he was following me around like an orphaned puppy after the kennel-keeper, when he punched me, quite hard, in the gut.

Chapter Twenty-Six

Someone was pressing something to my lips, urging me to drink. There was a buzzing in my ears, and a sound like drumming, and my heart hurt, and then a trembling, and a light so bright it forced my eyes to close...

The voices were coming from far, far away, but they were getting closer.

Someone was hurt? Or ill? Yes, that seemed to be the gist of it. I wondered who. It seemed pretty bad, they were groaning faintly, quite near to me. I tried to focus, but my head was still swimming and the voices got closer still.

I turned my face towards the voices and promptly threw up.

That cleared my head a little, enough so that I could hear the words more plainly.

"Drunk." That was Lannach, his voice laced with contempt.

"Not her. Not like this."

"Sure it is."

Guerin's face swam into focus.

"Caoimhe." He looked concerned. I thought he ought to worry about the person whose groans seemed so close, though. They didn't sound good.

"Let her sleep it off."

"This isn't how she is when she drinks." He was pulling me into a sitting position and there was the clink of pottery against my teeth and the sweet taste of clear, pure well water on my lips. "This is something else."

That was about the point when I realized the groans had been my own. My head was thick and aching, and my stomach hurt. I could see, though, that I was back in Rhwyn Keep, with no idea how I had gotten there.

I drank the water. My vision was clearing, and I saw that in addition to Lannach and Guerin, Arlais was here, too.

And Cowell. Memory returned in a rush. I sat bolt upright and said, incredulously, "You hit me!"

"Aye. Couldn't think of another way."

I fell back against the pillows again. No one else seemed to find his answer strange. Well, maybe Lannach. Yes, definitely Lannach. He had his aggrieved warrior face on.

"Don't even think about it," I said to him. "In a dozen years, I swear I only ever succeeded in landing a clean shot on him three times."

"Twice," said Cowell. "That first was a giveaway."

"Oh, thanks a lot."

"Well, why?" Lannach asked.

That was a good question. I was glad he'd asked it. I was fairly sure he wasn't going to get an answer, though. Or at least, not a good one.

"We needed to get her out of there." That was Arlais.

"And lucky you were there, too, lad. I'd have had a job dragging her back up here by myself."

I had closed my eyes, but at this, I opened them again, wide. I didn't think I'd ever heard Cowell admit to needing anything from anyone at all, much less to offer, however obliquely, something like a thank you.

"And you think I've mellowed," I said. He grinned.

"We think," said Guerin, and I could tell that he was measuring his words out carefully, like grain in a lean year, "that someone might have given her something, to make her seem drunk. Maybe they meant it for a joke, but maybe not. Maybe it was for something more."

"Robbery? Not one of us!" said Lannach, instantly insulted. "No one who serves the House of Machyll would even think it."

"No, no," Guerin said, hastily. "We didn't think that. It's something - er - local, we think."

"Yes, but - "

"There's always those who quarrel, even in a village." Cowell put this forward with a lot of authority for someone who hadn't actually done more than ride through a village on his way to somewhere else for at least forty years.

"You know the king is concerned about things here," Arlais said. "It could be connected with that."

And somehow, over the next few minutes, with many more similarly confusing and conciliatory words and some fairly blatant flattery, they got Lannach distracted into a happier mood. Finally, they eased him out the door, satisfied that he'd been a bit of a hero, and that everything was fine, under control, nothing to worry about at all.

It was a pretty good performance. I was impressed, although I wasn't sure why they had wanted him gone. I mean, I could guess why, but I couldn't be sure. And how these three had become allies in this was a puzzler, too. I lay back on the pillows, and watched them now, waiting to see where this would go.

Arlais perched herself on the edge of the bed, her face grave.

"Caoimhe, what can you remember?"

"Well, I had oatcakes and ale for breakf-" She glared at me. "Oh, all right. I was fine, I guess, until I'd been at the inn for a while. I was watching the dice...no, before that, I was thinking about - something, and I kept not being able to keep it in my head properly. And I was tired."

No one spoke. I thought about that tiredness, and how the light had glanced off the dice as they fell, little splintery sparks of reflected candle flames that I couldn't seem to take my eyes away from.

"Arlais? Did someone put something in my drink?" I couldn't see how that could have been. I'd been taking mine from the same pitcher as everyone else around me.

"It's possible." She didn't sound at all convincing, though.

I looked at her. I thought about what other things might be more "possible". I didn't like them very much.

"Caoimhe, you didn't take anything of Eardith's away from the cottage, did you?"

I said, with perfect, careful truth, "You saw what I took away. Why?"

"Someone," she said, "someone has searched this room. Twice, I think."

"Mine as well," said Guerin. "And at the cottage, well, it wasn't just a struggle that disordered things there, I think."

I thought back. He was right. Almost everything, chests, baskets, the little grain bin, they'd all been messed about.

"Well, what would they be looking for?" It was a risky thing to ask, I knew it, but I was curious about what Arlais might suspect.

She was canny, though. "I can't know that. It could be any number of things. But whatever it is, it is important to someone. Important enough that they would be willing to -" but then she broke off.

"Willing to poison me? Bespell me? It would be nice," I said, "if you would be a little more forthcoming, considering it's me they seem to be targeting."

"Forthcoming," said Cowell, "that's a bit of cheek, coming from you."

"What do you mean?"

"Well, where did you go this afternoon? How did you manage to slip past me? I knew just where you were since you stepped onto the practice ground this morning, and then suddenly you come wandering in from the yard without ever having left this room since you came in to change your shirt. So don't you," he finished, "pretend to an innocence you haven't had since you crawled out of your cradle."

"I can't help it if your spying skills are slipping, old man. There's a way out through the kitchen garden, you know." There was, too. The garden wasn't accessible from this room, not without going down through the main hall, but I was hoping Cowell wouldn't know that, offhand.

"And why would you have taken that way today?" He sounded suspicious, but not in a way that worried me.

"I fancied some of those early strawberries Lady Delwen grows. They aren't quite ripe yet, though, so I had to go off empty-handed."

They knew I was lying, of course. And they thought they knew why. I felt a little envious, actually. They didn't know how truly horrible things really were.

And my lie was working, in a way. They were disappointed in me, and suspicious and frustrated, but I could see that Arlais, at least, had given up on this line of questioning, and was thinking up some other way to deal with whatever it was that she thought was going on, and that Cowell was ready to abandon me to my probable bad end. I had no idea what Guerin thought. His face was blank and a little cold, as if he, too, was ready to wash his hands of me.

The moment passed. It was late, with midnight well behind us, and after an awkward silence, both Guerin and Cowell left, Arlais lay down on the pallet on the floor and I closed my eyes and listened to her as her breathing slowed, and eventually I fell asleep as well.

Chapter Twenty-Seven

I was just drifting up from a dreamless, fitful doze when I heard the door closing softly behind Arlais. The sunlight was streaming in and I could hear the cheerful sounds of Rhwyn manor starting its day.

I gave it a grain or two before I pushed back the blankets and swung myself out of the bed. There was a lot to do, and very little time.

They'd have to go it alone. They were safer without me and my guilty secrets, far, far safer. Everyone was. They'd be all right, I thought, once Ilona realized that I was well away, and she'd have to abandon her plans for me, whatever those had been. All I need do was to get free of Rhwyn Vale, and everything would be all right.

Or at least not as dire as if I stayed.

The first problem, of course, was Eardith's book. I would have ignored it, I would have forgotten its very existence if I could, but all I could think was that the danger of someone finding it was too great a risk. Anyone coming across something like that, chock full of arcane writing, was sure to give it to the most knowledgeable person there, and right now, that was Ilona. Even if it was found after she left, the idea that someone, anyone, might learn the secret of my birth was enough to get me scrambling into my boots, intent on sneaking down the hallway to the linens cupboard and then on to my well-deserved and long-delayed exile.

I put on my arming tunic and my mail shirt and stuffed my cloak into the saddlebags. I buckled on my sword and lengthened the strap on my shield and slung it over my back.

There was a girl hauling a bucket and mop down to a room at the other end of the corridor when I peeked out, but she was intent on her task. It wasn't so long before I heard her open a door and then close it behind her, and then I fairly ran to the cupboard.

It took two trips to get everything up into the loft, and then there was a nasty moment or two when I realized that I couldn't remember which dark corner I had stuffed the thrice-be-damned thing into. I found it, finally, and stuffed it into the saddlebags as well, and then it was another two trips to get myself and my belongings down to the ground.

The stable block was quiet. The entire courtyard was quiet. Most people were still scrounging cakes and ale in the hall, and the few souls about were people who knew me well enough. They wouldn't remark on my comings and goings unless someone asked. It seemed unlikely that anyone would, at least not for a little while.

I had been wrestling with the question of where to go for a good long while before sleep finally claimed me, but I thought I'd found the answer. The obvious way to a fast exit would be to head south, to Glaice or some other border fort, or, even, after that, west towards Kerris or beyond. The less obvious would be north to the nearest port, because real safety lay in getting as far from Dungarrow and Keraine as I possibly could.

But I had, in the chilly hours before dawn, thought of one other way, one that served every purpose, and seemed so unlikely and so perilous, to boot, that it might, I hoped, be some several glasses, perhaps even a day or two, before anyone thought of it. One that might give me just enough time to get well away from everything, and give them an easy out towards forgetting me.

If I could get as far as Dungarrow town unnoticed, and take ship to Fendrais or some other distant, foreign land, there was just the barest chance that I could limit the damage my existence had bred.

I rode down the lane and through the village at an easy pace, despite my urgency. It wouldn't do, I thought, to gallop around and cause anyone to wonder what I was about so early in the day. Look ordinary, I thought, look like nothing is important, like nothing is the matter at all. I even waved at Gair's wife as I passed her by the green, because it would have seemed odd for me not to.

I left the last outbuildings behind, and started along the northward curve of the road, and only then did I urge Balefire to a quicker pace, not because I thought I was free and clear, but because I had no desire at all to linger as I passed the shrine and the little path down to where Eardith's cottage had been replaced by a collapsed pile of still-smoking ash and charred beams.

We cantered along to the crest of the hill, where the road dropped gently down towards the crossroads.

149

And I didn't stop then, because it was too late. It was, in fact, something I might have expected: whatever luck I'd thought I might have had, I should have known it had run out long since.

There were already some riders waiting at the crossroads, and they had already seen me.

Chapter Twenty-Eight

They looked grim, standing there beside their horses at the side of the road. I guessed that my own expression wasn't much different. I stopped Balefire a few feet away, and just waited. They were bound to say something, eventually.

"And where were you off to, on such a pleasant morning?"

I was mildly surprised that it was Guerin who spoke first. Cowell was mainly the silent type as well, and I'd been expecting Arlais to be the one to break the ice.

There was a lot of ice, though, I guess. She was glaring at me as if I'd insulted her grandmother's cooking.

"Ah, well, it's been a long time since I saw Dungarrow in spring," I said, lightly.

He glanced over at Cowell. "That's five bits you owe me." He said it with satisfaction.

Cowell shrugged, saying nothing. He was waiting to see what Arlais would do, I realized with some shock. She was the one who was in charge here.

I thought suddenly just how much I'd underestimated her. She'd used my own preconceptions of her as a young, inexperienced, sheltered child, intelligent and learned, but weak and unschooled in the world, she'd used that impression against me. She'd taken those easy generalizations and acted them out, to keep her own counsel, to keep herself safe, while she watched, and listened, and come to her own conclusions.

I don't know if she had ever had Guerin hoodwinked, but she had fooled me, she had fooled Eardith, and she had fooled Ilona, too, if that condescending little show of flattery the other day had meant anything.

I really hoped it did. And I really hoped that Arlais could keep it up, because once Ilona knew anything for certain, it seemed likely that all nine hells would break loose at once.

I said, without much hope, "It would be best for everyone if you just let me go on."

"Really?" They said it, all three together, on an almost identical note of derision.

Guerin said, "That's your solution? To run away again?"

"Believe me, it's for the best."

"Why?" Arlais sounded quite honestly curious, not accusatory at all, and I thought that she knew too much, far, far too much already.

"It's better if you don't know. Trust me."

And that was a mistake. I knew it the moment the words left my mouth.

They pounced immediately, as if they'd just been waiting for it, all three of them, in a stream of outraged, determined, angry flow of confusion. I missed about half of it, but the gist was simple. That I was the one who had no faith, that there wasn't a single thing I'd done in days to gain their trust and that if I wanted their aid or even their silence in any way, I would have to come clean.

"All right," I said.

In the midst of the tirade, it had come to me how very weary of it all I was, how much I wanted to give up these burdens, how much I resented having to carry this load as if I actually had done something of my own will that had led me here. If they were so eager for knowledge, they could have it. I was done.

"All right." I slid out of the saddle and began to fumble with the buckle on my sword-side bag. I pulled out the book and handed it to Arlais.

"All right. But never say I haven't warned you."

She looked down at the little leather-bound thing.

"*Asarlaíoche.*" It came out on the softest of breaths, and then, at Guerin's sudden query, "A book you keep, for the harder knowledge. And... other things."

She had been standing on the verge, reins looped over her arm. Now she handed them off to Cowell without even a glance at him and took the book, almost reverently, and sat down on the marker stone at the side of the road. She opened the cover and began to read.

I said, "I don't suppose any of you brought any food? I didn't stop for breakfast."

Cowell grunted something ungracious and rather profane, but after a moment, he rummaged around in his scrip and produced a piece of hard biscuit and some dried meat. I'd been counting on his long experience as a soldier to have come prepared for every eventuality, and I said so. He looked angry still, for a moment or two, and then he bared his teeth in a sort of a smile and punched my arm.

"Idiot."

"So people keep saying." I was watching Arlais, deeply engrossed in her reading. She made a worried sound in her throat, and flipped a few pages back. Then she turned the book sideways and peered at something, frowning.

I took the biscuit and meat and led Balefire over to the far side of the road to let him browse among the early thistles. It wouldn't take her too much longer, I thought, gloomily. I wondered how much she would decide to share with the others. I tried not to think about their probable reaction to it, if she told them everything.

Guerin was leading Shadow over to join us. I tried to think of something to say, something that might not touch on anything too serious. Things would get serious enough, soon enough.

"Tell me. How did you know I would head for Dungarrow?"

"What? "

"How did you know I'd go back to Dungarrow?"

"Oh, that." He smiled. I tried to remember how much I hated that smile. "It wasn't so hard."

"Am I that predictable?"

"In a way." His smile grew. "I just thought of the most unlikely, boneheaded, obstinate thing anyone would choose if they were in your boots, the thing that could cause you the most pain and still gain your ends, and then laid odds that that was what you'd do."

His earlier annoyance had dropped away. He was relaxed and friendly, and tolerantly teasing, just as he'd always been with me.

Arlais was more than halfway through, now. It would only be a little while longer, I thought, before she came to the things I dreaded. A few grains of the glass before, perhaps, she would tell him what was written there, and that easy comradeship would be gone forever.

I tried not to think about how much that bothered me. Or why.

Be a rock. Be a stone. Be no living thing.

Arlais reached the last pages without moving, without her expression changing from the one she'd had throughout her reading: a puzzled frown of concentration, mixed with a growing excitement. I reckoned there were things in there that she thought she could use, explanations of rituals, or ancient lore, or new magics that she found enlightening, as well as the revelations about my birth and recent events. What she didn't have, when she closed the book and looked across at me, was any sign of revulsion or horror or fear.

I said, "You see? It would be better if I was gone from here long since."

"Caoimhe," she said, calmly. "You're wrong."

She stood. "Here," she said to the two men. "You both should read this, too. You need to know." She leafed through the pages to the ones I had learned to loathe. "Starting here. The other things, they won't mean anything to either of you, but these, yes, you'll need to read them."

She handed the thing to Cowell as Guerin crossed back over the road, and then she walked over to me.

"You cannot be serious," I said.

"I am perfectly serious," Arlais said, "Caoimhe. Listen to me."

"Why? You know what I am, now. What can you say? I should be gone, long since. I should be as far away from this place as I can possibly be. Or you should."

"Caoimhe, will you just listen for a moment? I think Eardith was wrong, at least in part."

"No, she wasn't," I said. "Hells, all my life, I've known it. From the moment I drew breath, I've been a curse for everyone around me. They die, or they come to grief or to evil some other way and *then* they die. I am misfortune for everything I come near."

"Caoimhe," Arlais said again. "Listen to me. You aren't evil. You aren't, not at all."

I could sympathize, I thought. Who would want to think they'd spent these last days shoulder to shoulder with a daughter of the Dark Incarnate?

"We need to face facts," I said, coldly. "I am that thing's disgusting utterance. Let's not spend our energy pretending I am not an abomination."

"You're wrong," she said, again. "Trust me in this, if nothing else. This is what I am good at, why they sent me here. It's one of my Talents. Eardith herself saw no evil in you, she says so. She tried to find it, to sense it in you, she expected to and she couldn't, and I cannot either. You might be the spawn of evil, but it isn't in you.

"Which," she added, "is damned peculiar, and I don't quite understand it, but it's true."

I shook my head.

"All my life," I said. "All my life tells me you are wrong, Arlais. Now let me go."

She wouldn't budge, though. After a while, I gave up arguing and instead led all four of the horses up over into the open field above the road and lay on my back watching the clouds scud by, while the others talked.

The two men, they wouldn't look at me, not directly, after they'd read what Eardith had written. The book had been handed back to Arlais, and I'd seen that my presence was making them all feel constrained and gone my way, but not too far, because Arlais was being so damned stubborn about me not just leaving them to face whatever was going on.

"You can't outrun your fate so easily," she'd said. "You'll just carry this with you, and it will curse you still. Why do you think Eardith left the book for you to find?"

"As a warning?" It was the only sensible explanation. But Eardith had had plenty of chances to send me packing, and hadn't done it. It seemed to me that she had regretted it at the end at least, though, and I said so.

Arlais just waved that away. She said severely that I should at least trust that she knew more of another holy one's reasoning than I did, and would I please just wait and let her work this problem out properly?

I couldn't tell what Guerin and Cowell thought about it. I had gone far enough away that I couldn't overhear their conversation. I didn't want to know how disgusted my very existence made them. Not yet.

And I was worried about other things, too. I was fairly sure that Ilona already knew the book existed, that she suspected that I knew now what I was, and that this would force things to a head before anyone had the time and knowledge to prepare for - for whatever it was that she would do.

And if she didn't yet know these things, what was to stop Cowell from telling her? I had no idea why, after decades of loyal service, he was suddenly being trusted to betray her. How did any of us know he was not her spy?

How did I know Arlais was not her creature, either? Or Guerin... but here, logic reasserted itself. If Guerin was playing false, then I might as well give myself up to madness right then.

And then, just as if I'd called his name out loud, Guerin was walking up the rise toward me. If he was really smart, I thought, he'd knife me in the ribs before ever I got my sword out of the scabbard. Aye, and then slit my throat and burn my bones, just to be on the safe side.

He did none of those things.

He sat down beside me, and he was silent for a good long while.

And then he smiled and said, "A hell of a day, isn't it?"

I laughed. I couldn't help it.

156

Chapter Twenty-Nine

We didn't speak much after that. We just sat there companionably watching the horses.

I didn't understand it.

Why was nothing changed for him? Why did he still see me as simply me, without doubts or shadows? He ought to have been keeping his distance and making signs against the evil eye. He ought, at least, to have been back on the road with Arlais and Cowell, arguing for stringing me up on the nearest tree or at least convincing them that the sooner I left Dungarrow and Keraine far behind me, the better for everyone. But he was doing none of those things. He just sat there, occasionally observing that the grass was taking on the green pretty early this year, and that Balefire looked fit.

And at long last, Arlais and Cowell walked up to where we sat, and I saw that Cowell, too, seemed perfectly comfortable sitting down with the demon-spawn.

This worried me all the more. I couldn't distrust him utterly, we'd known each other too long for that, but I couldn't put my full faith in him either. There were more mysteries here than I would have ever guessed at, even a seven-day past. I didn't like it, and finally I nerved myself up to say so.

He merely shrugged.

"No," I persisted. "You've taken her coin for years. Tell me why I should believe you don't feel any loyalty to her now, all of a sudden, like."

"She's killed before," he said, goaded. "She's turned good people into monsters and forced others to kill for her. And if I'd known all that before this spring, no power on earth would have made me accept so much as a beggar's bit she'd touched."

I don't know if I believed him, not entirely. His tone was bitter enough, but after this wholly uncharacteristic outburst, he was silent, refusing to tell me anything more, and I didn't see why, having decided his honour was at stake, he hadn't just left Ilona's service, instead of becoming an ally and spy for a priestess he'd known for less than three days.

"I still think me leaving here is safest for everyone," I said. "And we should burn that thing. If she wants it, for any reason, we should make damned sure she doesn't get it."

"That's the problem, Caoimhe. You can't destroy these things so easily. And Eardith was stronger in Gifts than most, and she spent years learning to hide things."

"Then give it to me and I'll toss it into the sea somewhere between here and Fendrais."

"You wouldn't get within ten leagues of the coast before Ilona caught up with you. The moment you run, she'll know that you know and she'll come after you. You saw what happened to you last night. And that's only because she suspects you know what you are."

"You've got an answer for everything, haven't you? For everything you want, at any rate. All right, then. What do you propose we do?"

It was lunacy, her solution was. It was idiocy and madness, it didn't have a ghost of a chance of working, and I said so.

That's the trouble with the holy ones, though.

Outsiders, ordinary folk, we don't know enough to argue these things decently. The holy ones, they just look at you with those pitying, superior eyes and explain, as if you were a toddler, that their reasons and methods wouldn't make sense to you, and that you must just put your faith in them because they know all those secret things the Mother entrusts only to them.

That was how they'd grown so rich. That was how they'd grasped power centuries ago, and maintained it for so long, unchallenged. The way they managed it, they could keep the rest of us ignorant whether we willed it or not, forcing us to take some of it, at least, on trust.

So when she said that she needed me there to break the protections, that she was sure Eardith had incorporated something of me or mine into the spell she'd laid on the thing just before she'd folded it into my second-best shirt, and that to break that part, Arlais would need my presence, well, I couldn't argue. Daft as it seemed, it was just the kind of thing Eardith would have done. What any servant of the Mother who had trained at the holy island would have done: used whatever or whomever came to hand, without a by-your-leave or a thank-you afterwards, because what else were we for, but to be used?

Arlais had plans for more than destroying the book. She knew how to do that, right enough, she said, but there were preparations to make, and the timing needed to be right. She didn't say, of course, that there were some things that Eardith had found or worked out, that she intended to either memorize or copy down in her own *asarlaíoche*, but I knew instinctively that she meant to.

She only needed a day or two to get things ready, Arlais said. There was a moonless night in two days' time, and that would be a night where her ability to break the protections and destroy the book would be greatest. Better still, she had found a way, she thought, to bind that thing up in the mountains, bind it so securely that even Ilona, be she never so wise, would not ever be able to find her way past those wardings.

If we could just stay that little bit ahead of Ilona for two days, she said. If we could just give her the chance to use her knowledge and craft her solution, then when I ran, it wouldn't matter so much. Whatever knowledge Eardith had found would be lost to Ilona, and Arlais would be free to force Ilona's hand, and cage that monster in the mountains more securely than ever. She'd be able to end this, for good and all.

There were a hundred questions I ought to have asked, and a hundred more I needed better answers to. I knew that.

There were a hundred reasons why none of what Arlais said was necessarily true and there were a hundred more why I shouldn't have trusted any of these people anyway, and I knew that, too.

But I hadn't slept or eaten properly for far too long, there were three of them there, presenting a united front, and the sun grew warmer, my stomach rumbled, and eventually I gave up the quarrel.

"Two days," I said. "I'll give you two days. And then I'm off, no matter what, Arlais."

Back at Rhwyn, Arlais solved the problem of getting my things back to our room without remark by the simple expedient of imperiously

159

ordering one of the village girls hanging around flirting with the soldiers from Keraine to take them upstairs for her.

And I went off to the practice ground, because at least this explained why I was fully armed so early in the day, and I attempted, for lack of anything better to do, to teach Lannach to throw a fake that any goatherd couldn't have predicted in their sleep.

Chapter Thirty

I dreamed deep that night, deeper and truer, maybe, than ever I had before. The holy ones, of course, put a lot of stock in dreams, but I never had. My dreams swayed between the impossible and the impenetrable, when they didn't veer into the horrific, and none had ever had the precision of truth.

But that night, I dreamed in a way that woke me gasping on a stifled scream of rage, a dream so strangely real and so hideously painful that I felt as if I were drowning in it, unable to find even the ghost of a hope to cling to. Not that hope had ever been a constant companion of mine, of course. But I had had glimpses of a world that had held its promise, at least, and now I felt none.

My cousin Iain, asking me mockingly if I wasn't tired? Wasn't I weary? Wasn't I?

And I was falling, now…

She spoke my name.

No. She cried it out, in fear and despair, and I was pounding on the door that lay between us.

And then it opened, showing me a weeping girl, who reached out to me in desperation, pleading, begging for something I could not give.

"She has my heart," she whispered. "She cut it out with the killing blade."

And then Feargal was there, pale and rotting, a gift from the grave.

"I didn't want this," he said. "I didn't do this. She made me as I am."

But my mother was there, too, angry and accusing, dragging her bloated green corpse behind her, all along the hallway at Penliath, and then the laughter sounded in my ears, so loud it blocked out everything else, until I turned and ran, kept running, as if I could somehow escape all this torment…

I lay in the dark, listening to the echoes of that dream, for a long, long time. I felt bruised and aching, as if I'd been sparring on the practice ground with someone much better than me, and I worked hard, in that hour before dawn, to wall myself up again, to close up every avenue of feeling, and to cloak myself in uncaring.

Be a rock. Be a wall of stone. Be no living thing.

After all, what good would feeling something do me now?

Chapter Thirty-One

The traders who unexpectedly arrived the next day weren't any of the ones who ordinarily came to Rhwyn.

It was early in the season, but this enterprising little group had heard that the Camrhyssi had been raiding the tiny villages and farmsteads that eked out their livings along the foothills, linked by the track running north from Ys Tearch. Against the odds, they'd decided there would be some extra coin to be made by bringing their wares along that way, ahead of the usual crowd. They'd followed Birais' forces at a fairly brisk pace, whilst driving hard bargains all along the way.

Consequently, they were in fine and cheerful moods to begin with, attitudes made all the more smug by Birais inviting them into the hall to quiz them personally for news from the south.

There wasn't much. Birais had left his younger brother in command at Glaice, and his wife, still holding court at Kerris, was known to be a brilliant administrator. There wasn't much they wouldn't be able to handle with ease. One bit of news did give us all pause, though.

The traders had lost a guard in an unprovoked attack by a wild pig, not five miles south of Rhwyn.

Too close for comfort, said Birais, but that was merely a convenient excuse. You could tell he was excited. We all were.

Everyone loves a boar hunt. The danger is high, but the return for success is high, too, and the traders seemed quite sure it was a sow. There might even be piglets, as well, and it was obvious, if the House of Machyll and his friends stayed here much longer, we'd all of us be down to living off bean soup and barley bread in a few more days. Not the sort of fare a king was used to.

The mood was contagious. Even the villagers who had come up to the manor to help out were getting into the spirit of the thing, reminiscing about a time some ten years back when a stag boar had run right through Rhwyn village and across the green and gotten stuck in the wattle fencing behind Derryth's garden.

"You aren't going," Arlais said to me.

"Of course, I'm going."

She frowned. "It isn't safe. And I might need you."

"Don't be ridiculous," I said. "It would look strange if I cried off. People would wonder. *She* might wonder."

Arlais had that determined, stubborn look on her face, but when she appealed to Guerin to talk sense to me, she was overruled immediately.

"If she doesn't go, it only draws attention to her, which is exactly what you said we didn't want. Don't worry, Arlais. I'll look out for her."

"I'm not the village's idiot child," I said. "I can manage a damned hunt without a minder."

And so, in the small hours before dawn, I got myself quietly dressed and armed, and down into the courtyard with everyone else. Birais had already sent a squad on ahead with Joss, to scout things out and get ready before the rest of us arrived.

"Be nice," said Guerin. "Stick close to me, so that Arlais can't complain."

"That worries you?"

"She might witch me into a tadpole."

We both laughed. It had been one of Einon's childhood nightmares, when he was very small, and he'd only admitted to it on a crazy, drunken night a few days after my fight with Mael. It was a private joke, one never spoke of it or even alluded to it if the young duke was within earshot, but it had become a kind of secret phrase for nonsensical dangers, for the few of us that had been present.

One of the king's friends was singing the "Lament of Caderyn" as we rode. He had a good voice, deep and melodic and it carried well, but it's one of those doleful, sad ballads filled with nothing but tragedy. It really didn't fit the occasion. It certainly wasn't helping my mood. Even so, it was a relief simply just to get out of Rhwyn.

It was probably only my imagination that made me sure that a pair of eyes were boring into my back everywhere I went. It was like a constant itch between my shoulder blades, even as we rode, and it made no sense. The Lady hadn't even come down for the evening meal yesterday, pleading a headache. I hadn't seen her for nearly two days, and more importantly, she hadn't seen me.

164

I really needed to take myself in hand, I thought, or I'd be seeing a troll in every tree trunk, as the saying goes.

The signs, according to Joss, were good. The air was still damp and foggy, especially in the low-lying places, but he said confidently that the sow seemed not to have gone far, and he thought there were others, which was natural. Wild ones still like to group together. Two stags, said Joss, and maybe three sows. He couldn't say how many had dropped their litters.

Meanwhile, he'd set up a feeder full of household scraps as bait, in a little clearing criss-crossed by several narrow game trails. The king divided us into smaller groups, four or five in each and Joss was finding stations for us, on the theory that there were only so many directions the pigs might go.

I was sent with Guerin and a couple of others to a spot on the northerly edge, where the slope alongside one of those little tracks rose gently back towards Rhwyn. It wasn't, I judged, terribly likely that any of the boars would run this way, but we had a pretty good view down into the clearing. It would be fun to watch, at least, once the morning mists burned away.

We waited. It's boring, of course, because you need to stay very quiet, but I didn't lack for things to mull over.

I could wonder what it was that was driving Arlais, and why she had not immediately sent word to Braide about the situation here. Or that maybe she had, but then there was the question of how she'd managed to do that. I thought I would have noticed, had anyone been missing.

She might have confided in the king, of course. If one of his soldiers had been sent off, I wouldn't know, except that no one was talking about a missing comrade, and troopers are notorious for gossip.

I could be suspicious of Lady Ilona's headache. It seemed nicely timed against my own revelations, and that could not be a good sign. I could wonder about how long she had been planning all this, but it seemed I knew the answer to that, deep down, and those thoughts hurt me far too much for me to examine them more closely.

I could wonder about the thing that had sired me.

But here, my mind rebelled completely. I could not imagine it, I could not envision it. Not without puking up what little breakfast I'd managed before we set out, anyway.

Strangely, this helped me, in a way. It occurred to me, in that forced, early morning delay, that my reaction bore out Arlais' assurance that I was not, in and of myself, evil. That whatever my disgusting origins, I still might not be an inherent abomination. I was still myself, whatever that was, and this cheered me, just a little.

There was a crackle of undergrowth, very faint, off to the east of us, and then, seemingly out of nowhere, we saw a huge stag boar, nosing its way through the trees from the south. It was only for a moment, and then the shape disappeared, swallowed up by the fog, which had not lifted. Indeed, it seemed to have thickened, rising up out of the little dell below us and deadening both sight and sound.

There were suddenly some crashing sounds, and a yelp of surprise or pain, I couldn't tell which. We were all of us on our feet, snatching up our spears, and then a pregnant sow came out of the trees below, barreling straight up that trail beside us, and we leapt from our hide and were after her.

It was stupid, what we did. We should have known better. We did know better. This wasn't the way it was supposed to go at all.

Within moments, I became separated from the others. The trail didn't allow room for all of us, and we'd spread out into the trees, rushing headlong after the beast, and even though I'd noted that the fog was still rising, that it had been steadily thickening, I didn't stop to consider that we were being idiots. I just ran, like everyone else.

For a long time, I could still hear them. I could still catch glimpses of them through the trees. There were flashes of intermittent sunlight on spearheads, there were shouts of excitement. There was an occasional bit of movement I only saw out of the corner of my eye, there was the sound of tree branches being pushed aside, the thump of feet through the underbrush, and occasional squeals of rage from the boar.

I was still running, not really caring where my feet were taking me, not noticing that the sounds from my companions were growing fainter, and unaware that I had no idea what direction I was heading. I saw, just frequently enough, those tell-tale markings to believe that I still followed my quarry and that the sow was not far away.

Even so, I was beginning to think I'd lost my goal, just beginning to sense that something was vaguely not right, when I saw the blood.

In a heartbeat I could feel the excitement coursing back through my veins. I was instantly certain it was a speared boar I followed, and I was off and running again. The blood wasn't in profusion. It was merely wounded, that boar, and I could think only of how good it would be to be in at the kill, and not of the danger a wounded and desperate animal can be when brought to bay.

But then the trail was fading, it was trickling away, it was gone, and so, gradually, I realized, was everyone else. The mist was still waist deep and swirling, enveloping me in it and slowly, as the blood drops disappeared into the trees, so, too, finally, did the thrill of the chase. My footsteps slowed and then halted, and I looked around me.

I was lost. Well, not entirely, I thought, considering everything. The trail had run more or less north and eastwards, as far as I could remember, and I didn't think that I had really strayed too far from that direction, overall. But with the fog, I couldn't say, in truth, that I knew where I was, or even how far I'd come.

I gazed up the slope. It seemed to me that there were clearer views if I got higher, maybe above the tree line, and from there I might be able to get a better idea of where the road was from here. Eventually, I reckoned, everyone else would make for the place where we'd left the horses, whether any of us had managed a kill or not.

The hill was steep. It took me some time to reach a place where my sight lines weren't obscured by mist or by the forest, and I was tired, far more tired than I expected to be. I leaned against a tree-trunk, to catch my breath.

When I finally looked around me and down into the valley below, I noticed three things.

The first thing I saw was how much time had passed. The sun was well past its apex and that made no sense. I couldn't possibly have been running after the sow for that long, could I?

The second thing I noticed was that the road was not visible from here at all.

And the third thing? The third thing was that I knew, roughly, where I was. And that was not a good place for me to be at all.

Chapter Thirty-Two

I felt no sense of panic. It seemed inevitable that, try as I might to change it, my course had been set long since. The choices had always been limited, and they had never been mine. There was no reason that this time should have been different.

Even so, I took a good look around, to see if there was any way I could avoid this. The terrain offered few options. And truly, I thought, this was no unfortunate happenstance. This had been carefully managed. I had been manipulated, certainly, and probably magicked into being here by someone or something that wanted things that only my existence could deliver.

You can't outrun your fate, Arlais had said. I wondered, then, if she had meant it as a warning or a persuasion. She hadn't seemed to want me to go on this little adventure, but I couldn't tell, at this point, if that had been a real fear based on secret knowledge, or simply a ruse, a way to deflect suspicion, knowing that I would go anyway, whatever she said.

I could, I surmised, try to scale down a bit of rocky scree I could see, just a little off to the west, a way that might let me down into the woods below, skirting the one place I wanted to avoid. It wasn't too terribly dangerous.

I could, of course, try to retrace my steps back down the mountain. It would be dark soon, and I would need to find some place to spend what would certainly be a cold and lonely night, and from there, I thought, I might even take the road south and escape, veiling my past and sinking into anonymity in some faraway place.

If I had learned anything these last few hours, though, it was that probably that none of these choices would do me any good. Something would happen to lead me back up towards that place where Joss and I had killed the wolves. I had, I was convinced, been witched in some fashion into coming here. It was obvious I had been witched before, when the need had arisen. I would probably be witched again, if it proved necessary, and the only things that running would net me at this point would be more tired, more resentful, more confused and thus more prone to poor judgment.

Running away, hiding away - I had done a fair bit of that, over the years. None of it had really served me all that well, in the end, had it? Maybe it was time to try a different tack.

This thing had found me, and pretty easily, too. There was really only one direction to go. Old Badb had been wrong. Ill winds didn't just follow me. They had been pushing me, all along, driving me like a ship into the shoals, all my life.

I wanted some control back. I might never have had much. I might have never had any, all things considered, but I wanted it now.

Even so, after everything, after a lifetime of suspicion and mistrust, I was not happy to see what was there in the ruins of that ancient temple, waiting for me. Unsurprised, but still unhappy, because it knocked away the very last spindly prop I had left.

Arlais lay, in an awkward, motionless heap, in the centre of the clearing, and the figure that stood over her was clearly not sorrowful about this.

There was no scent of blood in the air, no signs of violence, but I had seen death too often not to know it, even from a distance. Yet, I felt strangely unmoved, perhaps because I had turned this one over in my mind so often in the last day or so, it was only the finality of a suspicion confirmed. I had told her it was madness, and I had not been wrong. Whatever Arlais had tried to do, she had failed, and it had cost her.

It had cost everyone.

"You took your own sweet time," the figure standing over her said, crossly. "You should have been here long since."

I shrugged. Even I, with not a speck of the Mother's power or gift or talent of any kind, could feel the pull and swirl of sorcery around me.

How strong were they? One doesn't grow up surrounded by the gifted and the priestly without gaining some comprehension of how these things work. There are limits to the control and to the ability to force even one person to act against their own will.

They had had years of training, though, years of collecting forbidden lore, and years of practicing in secret how to wield their talents and their knowledge to the most efficient ends. They would have learned to mask those skills, not allowing anyone around them to know just how deeply they had gone into the abyss.

***

She had been one step ahead of me, all my life, had the Lady of Gorsedd.

She must have known what kind of hell I lived in, and therefore, when the time came, just the right blend of kindness and caring to apply that would leave me indebted and uncritical. She had bound me as tightly to her as she could have, and without the slightest of efforts, really. Even Meryn, and Meryn's obvious and increasing talents, and my devotion to Meryn, these had all just been useful tools.

She had had me there, right under her nose for years, and later, I realized, carefully watched and probably reported on and discussed, by both Iain and Feargal.

Not that I thought that Feargal, at least, would have been a willing spy. More likely, he'd have thought the same as me and assumed her questions were all ones born of affection and care.

Even after all he'd done, the hell he'd unleashed in one single night, I simply couldn't see Feargal as some kind of grand conspirator in this. And remembering those last days at Gorsedd, coupled with this new way of seeing Ilona's behavior, her every word and gesture now charged with a completely different meaning, it finally dawned on me that nothing about Feargal's actions or mood had been quite right, from that first night at Gorsedd onwards.

At first, nothing was different. With Feargal, nothing ever was. You could almost predict when he would come up with a joke, or a challenge, or a wild prank. But then, somewhere between the fourth bottle and when I'd finally gone off to bed, something had altered. I frowned, trying to remember.

He'd just gone suddenly, strangely quiet. And he'd seemed drunker than he ought to have been, he had a good head for drink, had Feargal, and he'd had a lot of practice. But he'd been staggering when we'd left the last tavern and made our rambling way back up to Gorsedd Keep.

And his eyes. No laughter in them, the next day, no *anything* in them, I thought suddenly, and then she'd come and taken him away and he'd been in her solar for hours, even though, and I remembered this with a shock, Ilona herself hadn't been in there, not the entire time, anyway.

In my mind, I could hear Iain's voice, asking me if I were too tired to come with them the second night, pushing through that odd, thick feeling in my head. I'd thought maybe I'd got a cold coming on, and stumbled off to my old room.

It had all, I saw now, been very carefully planned, and for a very long time. She had seemed to genuinely care for Meryn, at least, and Meryn for her but then, at the end, I realized now, that it was not so much me that Meryn had been avoiding, but Ilona.

***

"Come," she said. "There's a lot to do."

"What do you mean?" Keep her here, I thought. Keep her here talking and maybe something will happen to end this before it begins in earnest. What that might be, I had no clear idea. No one knew I was here. It seemed unlikely anyone knew that Arlais had come here. With Guerin goading him, Birais and Owain might worry enough to send out a few troopers to look for us, but there was no reason to think they'd come so far this way.

She looked at me suspiciously.

"Do not play the fool. You found Eardith's *asarlaíoche*. I know one of you must have, else it would still have been in that hovel you shared."

That was something, at least. Arlais had said she could keep it safe, and it seemed she had been right about this, if nothing else.

Ilona had a mad kind of faraway look in her eyes, now, fixed on her own goals and filled with a kind of anticipatory triumph. There was nothing else in the world for her, just now.

"I knew her so well. She would have written it down, all the secrets. She couldn't help herself - she was always trying to change things back, trying to "fix things", instead of grasping the nettle by the thorns and *using* what we won. I saw how it would be, from the very start. She never understood what truly matters. And I have waited too long and planned too much for this to delay any longer than I need."

If she sensed my fury, it didn't show. I reminded myself I should keep breathing.

Be a rock. Be stone.

"Did you," I asked, and I was astonished at how even and calm my voice was, "did you plan Meryn's death from the start?"

"Not at the start, no, not altogether…I thought her talents might be useful, you know. I would have been glad of them today. This all would have been so much easier. But then, she was so much like Eardith, really. Always wanting things to be right for people.

"I couldn't have ever let her go to Braide, in the end. She already suspected so much, Reverend Mother would have had the tale out of her in two grains of the glass. She was getting so hard to handle, too. She kept asking so many questions.

"So, I thought, why not be rid of them both? It wasn't as if I needed them anymore. It was so easy, really. Easy enough to trap Feargal, at least - stupid boy, no ambition, and he never wanted to believe in anyone's misdeeds. It could have been so different, if he had wanted more from life.

"And the power of it! There's so much power in a blood-death, Caoimhe, you know that better than anyone, I warrant. I gave her the reasons, and I gave her the knife, but the silly bitch, she thwarted me in the end, choosing the rope and no blood shed. I should never have taught her so much.

"But it hardly mattered, even so. It comes so easily to you, the killing does. Iain said he hardly had to do a thing, a mere word or three at just the right moment, to point you in the right direction. You did what you were born to do, and you'll do it again. You'll do it and that bitch on the island will live to serve me and watch, as all around her burns and dies. I'll see to that. *He'll* see to that. And then there will be power aplenty, for those of us with the courage to use it."

I swallowed, hard. It was not easy, being a rock. All I really wanted was to do was to kill her, the urge so great that for a moment, it was all I could do not to draw my sword and plunge it straight through her heart, but I was fairly sure she was prepared for that and that she had some spell up her sleeve to prevent this.

And even if I succeeded? What she had said about the power of a blood-death had the ring of truth. That thing could use it, twist even her death into a force for its own ends, I reckoned.

If Arlais had lived, there might have still been a way. If she was not lying there, so still, I might still have tried to end this here, because blood-magic, according to Arlais, was a wild thing, up for grabs the moment it was released into the world, and maybe she would have been able to catch hold of it, and use it for our ends instead. Her knowledge had given us hope, but that hope had died with her.

And Ilona's smile told me she knew what my silence betokened, or some of it, at least. The larger share, anyway. I listened to the sound of the wind in the trees below, and the echoes of other forest sounds, and did not let myself give in to anything so optimistic now.

"Come along," she said, again, and turned her back to me, utterly sure of herself. She walked north along the narrowing path, up into the heights above us, to the Well of Power, where that accursed thing that had sired me had remained through countless years, chained by ward upon ward, spell upon spell, waiting for us. Waiting for me.

It was like my dreams and nightmares all combined. Struggle as I might, I could not wake, and so I followed her. I couldn't really see what other choice I had.

Chapter Thirty-Three

It was a cavernous space, dark and drafty, with long, ominous shadows thrown up by the inadequate torches; a fugitive flicker that distorted the strange symbols carved into the rock, and for just a grain or two, I had the impression the place was empty.

But that was just for mere moments, until my eyes adjusted to the dimness and I saw those two figures, huddled up against what looked like a circular hearth. Only it wasn't smoke rising from it, but a sickly, green vapour as frail and insubstantial as ghost fingers, reaching up, endlessly seeking, and then they were sucked back down into one of those two dark forms.

I hadn't actually believed in this. Not really. Wells of Power had always seemed like the well-worn trimmings of every ancient tale, and even Ilona and her ravings hadn't brought the truth home to me.

And then that one huddled figure rose and changed, resolving itself into the man that had been inside the wolf the day that I'd killed it, so inhumanly beautiful, and so innately fell and dark and dangerous, and he smiled at me, and I thought my heart would stop right there.

"Hello, my child," he said and his voice was sweet, too, unbearably so, with the cadence of ancient music. In his eyes I saw that naked, predatory hunger.

I had been disgusted. I had been revolted, I had been angry and I had been frightened, too. I was merely terrified, now. The figure lying at his feet beside him, still unmoving, wore the red and gold. I couldn't see his face, but I knew him, a little.

Ordinary soldiers, they have a hard life. They risk their lives, time and again, and yet they aren't ever likely to be rich. They would be easy prey, be they never so honourable, if you gave them enough drinking money to do something that seemed only a prank, a wager, a jape, and I guessed easily how he'd been convinced to follow me, report on me, to slip me some charm or potion. Someone had been getting impatient, I suppose.

The sorcery was so overpowering now, you could almost reach out and touch it. It coiled and recoiled, braiding back on itself as it filtered out into the enormous, echoing space, but Ilona seemed not to even notice. Her entire being was completely focused on the Incarnate as if on a lover, her lips parted and glistening, her eyes shining with her desire.

"You see?" she breathed. "You see how I honour you, my lord? Do you see how I have brought all this to you, as I promised I would?"

He smiled at her, and then turned back to me, with a look of unholy amusement, as if we shared some special secret.

I wished he wouldn't. The thought that I was in any way a part of this, of him, was as sickening a thought as I could ever have had.

The Lady was on her knees, now, drawing out the circle, and he turned back to her. He began watching her with the single-minded enthrallment of a child too long denied a promised treat. If I had run, just then, I don't know that either of them would have noticed my absence.

How long this state of affairs would last, though, I couldn't be sure. She had spoken of blood magic and I thought, maybe, I could see how this would play out. I would kill this poor soldier, and then they would kill me, and all that blood and power of it might free that thing back into the world.

I remembered that odd scene, so many years ago, in the little shrine beneath Penliath. It had been about the same time of year, I thought. I hadn't known what my mother had meant to do, but I had known instinctively, even then, that it would have involved blood and death. My blood, and my death.

She hadn't known enough, my mother. She hadn't understood what this thing really wanted. Even if she had understood, she might well have misread it all anyway, through that lens of her own gaping neediness and greed, and simply gone ahead and done as she liked. She had never been a woman who could play a longer game.

And what a mistake it had been for my grandfather to intervene and save me. I could see that, now, that my end that day might have saved us all from a far worse fate.

Ilona finished the circle. She began to lay out the items they needed, the bits of old bone, the cups and the candles. Then she pulled out a flask of something viscous and dark, that she poured out into carefully placed pools at the five cardinal points inside the ring she'd drawn.

She lit the fluid and the little puddles smoldered, raising a stench of something honeyed and rotting, and it mingled above our heads with the smoke of the torches. She straightened back up, stepped away towards the Well at the centre of the circle she'd drawn, and waited.

The Incarnate produced an ancient, evil-looking, ritual knife, carved and dark, and handed it over to her. She held it reverently, with more than just a hint of fear, and after a moment, she began to whisper some odd, complex, unintelligible words in a sing-song chanting rhythm.

The knife began to take on a greyish glow, drinking in some of the ambient Power that still drifted from the Well. And it was drinking in hers, as well. Even I could see it, but the Lady of Gorsedd seemed strangely mesmerized and unaware.

The Incarnate sighed deeply, and looked back across the smooth stone flooring to me.

Ilona's voice grew louder. Beads of sweat appeared on her brow, and she swayed a little with the effort of this one final, all-important task.

It was Penliath all over again. All my life had dragged me here.

I wasn't a child anymore. It wasn't the circle, or these crazy rites, or even Ilona that frightened me now. It was that figure beside her. If once he touched me, I thought, that would be it. I could sense the power in him.

And I sensed something else, as well.

Oh, it wasn't that I had any gifts or talents. It was simply the training again, the training of a warrior, and it was something the holy and the wise always discount as too material, too obvious, too ordinary. It was just a function of observing and not trying to interpret past what was demonstrably present.

The Incarnate's Power was mainly, if not entirely, connected to the vapours still rising from that circle of stones. In the moments after he had stepped away, those hazy strings had still been reaching for him, clinging to him and melting into him, even as some of that power filled the knife or began spreading itself out into the cavern.

177

But the tendrils *were* diffusing now, that was the real point. They were beginning to drift away, and pretty aimlessly, too. They had begun to mix with the other forces at play here, almost at random.

The pair inside the circle turned to me, and that thing, he smiled at me once more.

There was a sort of faint sound, from very far away.

The two inside the circle, though, were so keenly focused on their own aims that neither of them seemed to notice.

They might, of course, at any moment, become aware of things beyond their little world. It seemed obvious that I needed to keep their attention on me and me alone, for as long as I could.

"Come," he said. "It's time for you to do your part."

I shook my head. I didn't trust myself to speak. My heart was like lead. I could not win, I realized, not against this. I could delay this, I might even be able to hamper their ends, but winning? No.

I could feel a crushing despair, and the weight of too much magic and power in this place, like a millstone on my chest, pressing ever harder against me. It hurt even to breathe.

"Come into the circle," he said. "Come to me, kill for me, and I swear, your fate will be mighty beyond dreams. You belong to me."

And my body - it wanted to. It was straining to go. It took everything in me not to move, not to do as I was asked.

I took a deep, painful breath and said, "You lie." I could feel it, the mockery and the triumph in them both. That circle encompassed my death, at least, if not something far worse.

The theft of a daughter cuts at the roots of the world.

Where had I heard that? Was it only a rhyme out of some old fireside story, or something more? It seemed an important truth, it seemed like the heart of the thing, but I couldn't think why.

My head felt thick and clouded. Far away, from a place as muffled and distant as a dream, I heard voices, shouting, but I wasn't able to tell anymore if it were echoes from some faraway imagining, or if there still were other people left in this world.

"Take her," said Ilona, breathlessly. "Bend her to your will, my lord. Time is short."

Chapter Thirty-Four

It was suddenly so quiet now, I couldn't even hear my own breathing. It was as if the rest of the Mother's creation had fallen away, leaving only the three of us alone and frozen at the end of the world.

"Kill him." The Incarnate's tone was perfunctory, almost disinterested.

"No." It hurt, that single syllable.

"Why not? What is he to you but a traitor? He needs to die."

It was actually funny, in a way. Father and child, getting to know one another at last.

I shrugged. The weight against my chest pressed harder.

He said, still confident, "You will do it, you know."

"Why should I?" I could barely draw breath, now, but it seemed important not to show that.

"Because I will it. Because you were born for this. Because you belong to me."

"And if I refuse?"

"Why should you? You have killed for others before, and with much less to gain." I considered this. He seemed very sure of me, even now.

"If you do not kill him," the Incarnate said, "he will die anyway, they all will, and you with them."

Well, that had the ring of truth, at any rate. I sucked in more air, no longer caring about the pain.

"Everyone dies." I said, at length. "Rich women or poor farmers, babies and greyhaired grannies, they do it every day. Now or tomorrow or a hundred years on: there's no difference, not for him, not for me, not for anyone."

He watched me through the mottled light, eyes now narrowed and suspicious, probing.

"Do your own damned dirty work," I said.

He shifted so suddenly, in a single movement so swift, I had no time to even realize he had done so.

The Incarnate touched me and screamed, and his fingernails, suddenly as long and sharp as eagle's talons, ripped along my arm, leaving a thread of intense and burning agony in their wake. He spun, and his hand connected brutally with Ilona's cheek, sending her stumbling out of the circle. She collapsed in a heap, moaning.

"Liar!" He was screaming still. "Liar! You swore she was mine!"

Ilona raised her head. "She *is* yours! Who else could have fathered her? I made sure that oaf the little fool was dallying with was as barren as a wethered ram - why else should I have let him come with us?"

He spat at her, and said something foul, and she shrieked in pain, her head falling back onto the smooth stones with a sickening thud.

He looked back to me.

He raised his hands.

The threads of vapour, still leaking from the Well, ran suddenly straight and true, right into him, and I braced myself. I couldn't hope to withstand this, but I could try. I could hold on a little and not shed anyone's blood, and maybe that would be enough.

And then suddenly, I was falling, my body hitting the hard stone floor, as someone careened into me like a boulder out of a catapult, smashing into my side and knocking what breath I still had right out of me. I rolled over and struggled to my feet, and this time my despair was not magically induced, but something real and all my own.

What in the name of every hell had Guerin been thinking? I could have hit him, I was so furious, except that he was out of my reach. His momentum had sent him sprawling across the cavern into that chalk-drawn circle, right past Ilona and not a hand's span from the curving line of stones that marked the Well.

In an instant, Ilona was on him, grasping at his throat and trying to choke him. She was gasping for breath, they both were, I could see them locked into a fearsome struggle, and while I had thought her a powerful mage, one part of me noticed that all the force and strength in her was gone. That knife that the Incarnate had given her had sucked it all away. It lay abandoned on the floor, still glowing with that unholy grey heat.

Ilona looked desperate, and nearly spent by her efforts so far, and yet she still was latched on to Guerin's throat with the ferocity of a mountain cat, and the pair of them rolled away, out to the edge of the circle.

I could do nothing for him, I knew that. And if I couldn't find a way to change all this, it wouldn't matter much, anyway.

I looked across the cavern. I couldn't even see the walls at all anymore. They had disappeared into the swell of power surging around us.

The Incarnate looked, too, and just for a moment I would have sworn the barest uncertainty crossed his face.

I was wrong, I suppose.

Into that unearthly silence, he began to laugh.

"Did you think your little stratagems might save you?"

He lifted a hand and the sorcery that had grown out around us lifted high, compacting in on itself and like a snake, it twisted and writhed above our heads.

Now I could see that Guerin had not come alone, although he might as well have, for all the good it would do.

The people at the entrance of the cave were caught, entangled in some arcane trickery, frozen in that same despair he'd locked on me. I could see them clearly, though I couldn't imagine how they'd known to come here. Cowell, and Birais and Lannach, and even some others I didn't know, struggling furiously against a wall of terror and anger.

Useless: not a priestly talent or a gifted among them. I was on my own, which was more than ordinarily depressing.

I had a choice to make. I had told Arlais, once, that my death didn't matter. That winning was defined by my opponent's death only. I didn't need to survive to be victorious.

The trouble was that this time, I was making that choice for everyone else, too.

Be a rock. Be a wall of stone. Be no living thing.

Or not.

I moved as fast as I could, scooping up the knife where Ilona had dropped it, and slashing wildly at the Incarnate.

It had the virtue of surprise, at least. The knife ripped across his chest, and then I felt the vibration and the pain, and I stumbled and rolled with it, past them all, past the Incarnate, Ilona and Guerin, past the still-unmoving body of that nameless soldier.

And then I dropped the damned thing into the Well.

Chapter Thirty-Five

There was a moment, between my fingers letting go and the sound of that obsidian blade clattering against something unseen down inside the Well, a moment where I actually thought I might get away with this.

And then all that sorcery, all that greenish vapour and wild, arcane force that had been pouring out into this place, held at bay and biding its time, it all rushed back in on itself, following the knife into the Well, and leaving a kind of airless, empty hush of death behind it.

Only for the briefest of moments.

Then something spat it all back up, and that was not at all a good thing.

It wasn't sound, although that might be the only word you could put to it.

It wasn't movement, although I felt it, shaking deep within me, a roaring pulsation from somewhere far inside the bowels of the earth.

It wasn't even painful, so I didn't quite understand why there was so much agony involved.

The shock of it had flung me back away from the Well, and I was not aware of very much else, except that the Incarnate, in that instant after he and Ilona both scrambled over and past me to the Well's stone edges, the Incarnate was howling with an inhuman fury.

The torches had been snuffed out in an instant, but all that force, in its sudden return, it lit us up like ghostly green fire, and I saw that whatever had held it, it was loose now, and raging like a tempest, crackling against the rock walls and showering me in a murderous hail of cold, black sparks.

I looked back to the Well, the source of this infernal torment, and saw the two of them still scrabbling at the edge, blind to everything but their own greed, and I saw that poor, unnamed soldier rise, and heard him speak.

But not with his own voice.

"GetoutGetoutGetout!'"

That was - Arlais? If I hadn't been on the ground already, it might have felled me with the shock.

The soldier-Arlais shrieked her warning again, and I felt a strong hand pulling me up, dragging me by force back toward the entrance, and I heard soldier-Arlais screaming something odd and terrible that I didn't understand.

And then I found my feet again and was running, too, following Guerin and Birais and the rest of them, all of us plunging blindly down the smooth-walled passageway and through the narrow, rocky gorge and away, out into the green, grassy place where the weathered stones of an ancient ruined temple still lay, rooted forever into the earth.

Chapter Thirty-Six

I asked her, a long time later, how she'd done that. How do you die, but not die?

"It's a simple enough trick," she said, airily. "It's just a little of this and a little of that, really, things that make up every spell. Any student at Braide could tell you that. But then, Ilona was always so sure that ordinary magics were pointless, she never paid any attention to how they work."

I asked her a lot of other things, too, like how she had been able to count on me to do the one thing that I had done, when she had been nearly a half-mile away, or how she had known any of it would work at all. And I got equally vague answers that really weren't answers at all.

But that was later.

***

Out in the world, it was still deep night and there was fresh clean air and velvet darkness. I leaned wearily against a gnarled old ash tree and wondered how I had lived for so long and never noticed how good this world could feel.

Cowell came by, and I thought he might punch me in my arm again, but then he thought better of it, and just shook his head and said I was a Goddess-be-damned fool and he was glad of it.

Guerin was still beside me. He told me to sit, and I ignored him and just concentrated on how sweet the night air felt as it slid into my lungs.

Lannach came by, and shook my hand and said something about courage.

"That wasn't courage," I said. "That was just stupidity that didn't go all arse backwards, for a change."

And then I said, because it had become annoying, "Don't fuss, Guerin. It's the merest scratch. Let it alone."

Guerin stopped pawing at my arm.

"Was there something," he inquired, "that you particularly wanted to bleed on? I'm willing to arrange it."

I looked. He wasn't joking, not utterly. The gashes on my arm were deep and the red blood had soaked down my sleeve right to my wrist. I would need a new shirt.

"It is a bit pig-like, isn't it? Sorry."

The King of Keraine was laughing at us, a little. But then, when Guerin had convinced me to sit, finally, and managed a makeshift bandage, Birais stopped laughing and said to me that he was greatly in my debt.

He was extremely serious.

"Lannach has the right of it, even so." He said this with an emphasis that wouldn't allow for any flip remarks. To be honest, I had no desire to make a joke of this. I was much too tired. "You never wavered."

I had wavered plenty, as I recalled. But I couldn't think of how to explain what I'd done, or why, and finally I just muttered that it was really Arlais who had saved us.

"You gave her time to work in."

That had been sheer bloody-mindedness, really. It wasn't as if I had known what she was doing. But I couldn't say that, either. Not with him looking at me with so much admiration. Admiration and something else, something I had seen in other people's eyes, but never, ever, not even once, directed at me.

Daughters are the roots of the world. I suppose he had learned this catchphrase, too.

"Any man would be proud -"

"Don't," I said. I closed my eyes against this onslaught.

I couldn't take this, not now. I didn't want this. I didn't need this.

And he certainly didn't need it either. He already had heirs. True, attested, blood-heirs. No one needed to muddy those waters now.

"Don't. Please. It's enough that - that you and I know what I am. And what I am not."

To this day, I don't know if it was relief or disappointment that he felt then. But he let it be, after that.

It was so peaceful, now. I wanted nothing more than for that peace to last.

It couldn't, of course. This was just a tiny grain of calm and quiet that would end soon enough. Once the sun rose, we'd have that long walk back down to Rhwyn Vale, and then there would have to be explanations, and actions, and changes. All those old uncertainties would come crowding in.

Guerin sat down beside me.

"What will you do?" he asked. He had a knack for uncomfortable questions, Guerin had.

I shrugged.

"You could go back, you know. He misses you. He would find a way to daub over the cracks, if you give him the chance."

"I can't." I said. "I can't do that anymore. Kill to order, I mean. I - I want these things to mean something, if they have to happen at all. I want them to mean something to me, I guess. And besides, Einon doesn't need me, or anyone else, to act for him. He's not a boy, anymore. It's better that he rules alone."

"Will you stay on here, then?"

I considered that.

"Owain doesn't need me either. Nor Delwen. They've borne the weight of this for too long, without the right to make it their own. Someone in Birais' entourage must know the proper form for deeding lands over to a faithful vassal. I'll have to see that done before I go."

"And after that?"

"I have no idea. There's always that ship to Fendrais, though." And I fell silent, because the appeal of exile, never that great, was gone entirely now.

"Well," Guerin said, eventually, "You could come to Orleigh, you know. There will always be a place there for someone with courage and honour, who knows what really counts."

I turned my head, and tilted it back to look at him.

"Are you," and I heard just the slightest tremor of amusement in my own voice, "Are you offering me a job?"

"Idiot," he said. "I'm offering you a *life*, Caoimhe."

I didn't think I was the real idiot here, and I said so. He disagreed.

"I'm bloody hell to live with," I said. "You wouldn't have a moment's comfort again, ever."

"I'll take my chances. I'm not precisely anyone's golden hero of legend, either, Caoimhe."

"No," I agreed. "What in the name of every filthy demon of hell possessed you to crash into me back there, come to think of it? If that's the kind of behavior you engage in normally, it will be a pretty short marriage. You're likely to die before you're thirty, doing things like that."

We'd forgotten we weren't alone. Well, I had, anyway.

All of them, kings, witches and nameless soldiers, were having a fine laugh at our expense.

Apparently, neither of us cared.

Epilogue

It was silent now, a kind of quiet he knew only too well. He'd had long years, tens and tens and tens of years of that quiet. He had begged for forgiveness, he had begged for release, and he had cursed the old hag, too, he had cursed the darkness, but nothing had ever changed.

Nothing, until the witch had come to him, with her shallow little dreams of dominance, and he'd convinced her so easily of a better way. It had been effortless, really, she'd done most of the persuasion herself. A word here, a hint there, and she'd run headlong into his plans. She'd been so willing, so eager to betray anyone and anything for the promise of greatness, and never once had she doubted his willingness to share the Power, the stupid cow.

And so he'd told her where to look for answers, told her what to do, even told her what sort of vessel to look for, where he could plant the seed of destruction best.

But now, when the screaming finally stopped, he had known the bitter truth. He flung the corpse away in disgust, because it had done its work, after a fashion. It had not been enough.

He was free, oh yes…and yet, not free. He had thought it might have worked, there at the end, to suck out the life from that hapless boy the bitch had brought him, and in a way, he'd been right. In that moment of Changing, he'd spoken Words of great power, that no one but he alone in this world today knew, and for just a single grain of the glass, he thought that he might have done a Thing that no other mortal had ever accomplished.

Well, and so he was free, indeed, free to wander, impotent and ruined, a kind of shadow, without the threads of power that the Well provided, should he leave it for too long.

Too late, he'd seen the danger. Too late, when that seeking force latched onto this horrid little clinging human groveling at his feet, and the Changing spells had caught her, too, and shared with her that single tie to the Well, even as she was caught in the binding spells. And now she was reaching deep, scrabbling for the Power, disbelieving, not understanding what her fate now truly was.

She was drinking it in, in the blind hope that enough might free her. He remembered that he had done that, too, long ago. He could have told her it was useless, and a trap, but then, why should he?

Hers had been the original mistake, after all, for not making sure that the little sow wasn't playing her lover false and was pregnant with another man's child already. She should have made sure of the girl.

He shouldered her aside. He still retained the need, and he was still the stronger one here. He was aware, even as he drew in the forces, that they were no longer as truly his as they had been, that in fact she had as much right to them now as he, but she did not know that, and she gave way without a murmur, crawling a little way off and hugging herself to herself, waiting till he might let her take them in again.

And so the cavern was dark again and silent as it always was, mostly, and time slipped by unnoticed, and they grew fat with the pleasure of the Well, nursing their angers, and they grew stronger, both of them, or so they believed.

And it came to them both, after a time, that there might be another way, to have the vengeances they craved and to be truly free.

The End

About the author:

Morgan Smith has been a goatherd, a landscaper, a weaver, a bookstore owner and archaeologist, and she will drop everything to travel anywhere, on the flimsiest of pretexts. Writing is something she has been doing all her life, though, one way or another, and now she thinks she might actually have something to say.

But if you really want to know more, download "Flashbacks (an unreliable memoir of the '60s)".

Discover other titles by Morgan Smith

A Spell in the Country

Flashbacks (an unreliable memoir of the '60s)